MAKE ME
Yours

Kendall Ryan is the *New York Times* and *USA Today* bestselling author of contemporary romance novels, including *Hard to Love*, *Unravel Me*, *Resisting Her* and the *Filthy Beautiful Lies* series.

She's a sassy, yet polite Midwestern girl with a deep love of books, and a slight addiction to lipgloss. She lives in Minneapolis with her adorable husband and two baby sons, and enjoys cooking, hiking, being active, and reading. Find out more at www.kendallryanbooks.com

Also by Kendall Ryan

MAKE ME
Yours

Kendall Ryan

HARPER

This novel is entirely a work of fiction.
The names, characters and incidents portrayed in it are
the work of the author's imagination. Any resemblance to
actual persons, living or dead, events or localities is
entirely coincidental.

Harper
An imprint of HarperCollins*Publishers*
1 London Bridge Street
London SE1 9FG

www.harpercollins.co.uk

A Paperback Original 2015
1

A catalogue record for this book
is available from the British Library

ISBN: 978-0-00-813402-0

Chapter 1

No matter how you sliced it, being the third wheel sucked. I scooted to the opposite edge of the picnic blanket, eager to distance myself from Ashlyn and Aiden's very public display of affection. I reached my limit when Aiden leaned over my friend and hand fed her a strawberry, kissing her lips as she chewed.

Gag me.

They'd been dating for a year now after meeting during an amnesia research study. Aiden was the patient and Ashlyn, as a fellow Ph.D. student, was studying him. It was considered risqué at the time, but I'd come to accept that they were good together. That didn't mean that they weren't sometimes nauseating to be around. I put up with it because I loved Ashlyn like a sister, and she was happy. However that didn't mean I needed to be cock-blocked by them at every turn. And the cutie playing football in the park with his equally delicious friend was my next victim.

I threw a grape at Ashlyn to get her attention. She was somewhat distracted, with her tongue currently lodged inside Aiden's mouth. The grape bounced off the back of her head and she turned to me, confused.

'Hey, look at that fine piece of man meat. Two o'clock.' I tilted my head, motioning to her right.

Ashlyn snuck a glance and grinned. 'The blonde? Blue shorts?'

I nodded. He threw the football through the air in a perfect spiral and into the waiting hands of his friend.

'He looks a little young,' she said.

I rolled my eyes. 'His friend's not bad either. Both of them together might be fun.'

'Just be safe.' She shrugged and gave me a wink. 'Go for it, babe. We'll wait here.'

I hadn't even had time to think about my next move when the ball Mr. Adorable and his friend were throwing landed at my feet. This would be easier than I thought. Like taking candy from a baby.

I stood and brushed off my jeans, leaning over casually to retrieve the football. With it tucked against my hip, I sauntered toward them. They watched me approach. The friend was smiling, but Mr. Adorable was more guarded.

'I think you dropped this.' I tossed the ball into his capable hands. He caught it easily. Thanks to my older brother, I actually knew how to throw a football. I figured he'd invite me into their game, or make some suggestive comment about touching his ball, but instead he just smiled.

'Thanks.' He turned and tossed the ball to his friend who was still watching me and missed the pass entirely.

Are. You. Kidding. Me?

Whatever. Rejected, I walked back to the picnic blanket and slumped down.

Ashlyn caught my mood and shifted closer to me, abandoning Aiden for the moment. 'Are you seeing Professor Gibson tonight?' she asked, trying to draw me into a conversation. I appreciated her effort to distract me from that epic fail as well as keeping me from feeling like I was intruding on a private moment between them.

'Nope. He has his son tonight. And call him Stu—'Professor Gibson' is just creepy.'

2

'Have you met his son?' Aiden asked.

'Definitely not. We're not dating. We're fucking,' I clarified.

'All righty then,' Ashlyn laughed and shook her head. 'You're more emotionally damaged than I ever realized.'

'It works for me.' I shrugged. It was the simple truth. I wasn't looking for a relationship and Stu, whose divorce was still fresh, certainly wasn't either. It was the perfect arrangement. He was thirty-six, recently single with a four-year-old son, and a professor in the business college, so our paths didn't cross in the academic world. Which was good. It kept things from getting complicated. We had good sex. It was as simple as that. I'd met him at a charity function the university sponsored and I'd been seeing him a couple times a week for the last month. It was nice, regular sex with a nice, normal guy without any drama or expectations beyond enjoying the moment. Okay, so it was my twisted version of perfect, but I knew it was all I was prepared to handle at the moment.

After a few more unsatisfying minutes of watching Ashlyn cuddle with Aiden and being ignored by the guys on the lawn, I grabbed my purse and told them I was taking off, getting a vague, halfhearted wave goodbye in return.

It wasn't a long walk back, just a few short blocks. Not even enough time to dig my cell phone out of my purse to distract me.

I rented a large townhome on a sizable corner lot in a beautiful neighborhood in the city. I had the first and second floors all to myself and I knew the owner had been slowly been working to restore the remainder of the building—the top floor—to its former 1920s elegance.

Rapid footsteps coming up behind me caught my attention, and I spun around. The cutie from the park was jogging in my direction.

Aw, he'd come to make amends. He probably just didn't want to share me with his friend.

I had reached the wrought iron gate at the walkway to my townhouse, so I stopped and waited, placing my hand on my hip, watching as he sprinted the last few paces.

He had stripped off his T-shirt and was now in just a pair of gym shorts slung low on his hips and running shoes. His chest and stomach were smooth and toned, reminding me strangely of one of those kids' slip-n-slide water-play toys. He slowed to a stop and bent over, resting his hands on his knees. His chest rose and fell with each deep breath, pulling me into a trance as I watched.

I was formulating a witty opening line when he rose up and looked at me. His eyes were a gorgeous shade of deep blue, and his summer tan had yet to fade away, giving his skin a nice golden glow. He held the football under one arm and his T-shirt bunched up in the other hand. He could have been a freaking Ralph Lauren model. I didn't often feel out of place, or lost for words, but he had me flushed and momentarily silenced by just his dominating physical presence.

He rose to his full height—standing several inches above me. I smiled up at him and pulled in a breath, recovering slightly. 'Stalking me now?'

His eyebrows pulled together in confusion. 'Oh, right. You're the girl from the park.'

No shit.

'I live here,' he said haltingly, still trying to catch his breath.

'You live where?' I asked, seeing as how we were standing in front of my house.

'Up there.' He pointed to the third floor, with its steeply pitched roof and minuscule octagon window.

'Someone can live up there?' I didn't mean for my face to scrunch up in repulsion, but when I saw his expression fall, I knew I had offended him.

'Not someone. Me. And yes, I live there. It's small, but it's clean and it's enough.'

I had no idea that the attic space was for rent. No one had lived up there in the two years I'd rented the house. 'Oh,' I said, recovering. 'I guess we're neighbors then—I'm the first and second floors.'

He glanced at the house again, with its wide front porch, big wooden door and spacious layout. 'All that? Just for you?'

I nodded. It was too much for one person, but I liked having my space. And since my parents had both funneled a large sum of money into my savings account to keep it away from each other in their divorce, I might as well live somewhere I liked. I'd decorated it with simple, yet stylish furnishings that I'd loved bargain hunting for. My townhome could now rival an upscale furniture catalog.

'Well, I guess I'd better go up and grab a shower. It was nice meeting you…'

'Liz.'

He smiled. 'I'm Cohen. And since we're neighbors, let me know if you ever need anything.'

'Sure. Likewise.' I returned his easy smile and watched his sexy back as he made his way around the side of the house to the staircase leading to his door. Oh yeah, I'd be looking forward to needing his help one day soon.

Chapter 2

I stayed up too late working on a research paper, skipped dinner and instead fueled up on a bottle of red wine and a bar of dark chocolate with sea salt, my all-time favorite. By the time I fell into bed, I was exhausted and still slightly buzzed. Which is why when I woke up suddenly a couple of hours later, I didn't trust that my eyes were working properly.

A dark object swooped and circled above my bed, casting bizarre shadows in the moonlit room. What the…?

The object stopped moving and perched itself on the edge of the light fixture hanging from my ceiling. I blinked rapidly and squinted in an attempt to see more clearly. Then it stretched out a pair of wings and I let out a shriek. It was a bat!

I jumped from the bed, kicking my way free from the covers. I ran from my bedroom like I was fleeing a crime scene and only stopped when I was standing on the front porch, my heart thundering in my chest.

I rolled my shoulders back, trying to shake the creepy-crawling feeling from my skin. I looked down at my bare feet, realizing I was outside, dressed in just a black tank top and tiny pink shorts in the middle of the night. Not the smartest move. A dog barking in the distance brought my attention back the moment, and figuring out what to do next.

It was too late to call the landlord. My cats were worthless and couldn't be counted on to kill a spider, let alone catch a bat. Maybe I could go upstairs and ask my hot new neighbor to come deal with the animal. He'd said to let him know if I needed anything, and I figured this definitely qualified.

But I couldn't venture up to his apartment dressed in practically nothing. I gave myself a pep talk and dashed inside, grabbing a pair of jeans from a laundry basket in the hall and sprinted back to the porch, slamming the door behind me. I quickly stepped into the jeans and pulled them up my legs, buttoning them overtop of the shorts.

I straightened my shoulders and marched up the stairs to Cohen's third-floor apartment. It was cool outside and the wooden steps under my bare feet sent a chill up my spine. Well that, and the idea of waking a complete stranger in the middle of the night to ask for a favor. But I had no other choice. There was no way I could go back into my apartment, let alone go back to sleep with a bat flying around in there.

I reached his door. It was the same solid dark wood as mine, with a decorative brass knocker in the center. I knocked on the door loud enough to wake him. I wasn't sure if he was a heavy sleeper, but I didn't want to take the chance. I normally felt safe in my neighborhood, but the combination of waking up to an animal in my room combined with being outside at this hour lent a creepy vibe I couldn't shake.

I was about to knock again when the door opened and a sleepy, shirtless Cohen stood before me.

'Liz?' he croaked.

'Can I come in?'

He moved away from the threshold so I could come inside. 'Did something happen? What's wrong?'

I nodded and paced his tiny living room. 'There's a bat. Downstairs.' I pointed to the floor.

'In your apartment?'

I nodded again.

'Christ.' He ran his hands over his face. 'Okay. Wait here. I'll take care of it.'

He retreated to what I assumed was his bedroom and returned a minute later dressed in jeans and a fitted gray T-shirt. His hair was rumpled from sleep and he looked adorable.

'What are you going to do?' I asked, hoping he had previous experience in bat removal.

'I don't know.' He went to the closet near the front door and pulled out a tennis racquet.

'Wait.' I jogged to his kitchen and grabbed a pair of oven mitts from near the stove and a plastic shopping bag from the counter. 'Here.'

I handed them to him. He put on the oven mitts and held the tennis racquet defensively in one hand, the plastic bag in the other.

'Okay. You're ready.'

We both laughed at the ridiculousness of this situation.

'Just sit tight. I've got this.'

I grinned at his confidence. 'Thank you.'

He nodded and disappeared out the door.

I bit my lip and I hoped he wasn't mad about me waking him up. But the way he'd laughed about the oven mitts before heading downstairs put me at ease. I sunk down onto his couch and waited.

His apartment was tiny, but it was clean and neat, and furnished simply with comfortable pieces. The living room consisted of a worn leather couch, along with a beat up trunk for a coffee table. His dining nook held a round kitchen table laden with various textbooks stacked in piles and was surrounded by several mismatched chairs. Definitely homey and inviting.

A few minutes later, Cohen was back.

'Well?' I jumped to my feet.

He shook his head. 'I couldn't find the little bastard.'

For just a moment I wondered if I had dreamed the bat, but no, I was certain I hadn't.

He shucked off the oven mitts and returned the tennis racquet to the closet by the door. 'I assume neither of us will be getting back to sleep now,' he mumbled, running a hand along the back of his neck.

'Sorry about that.'

He met my eyes. 'Don't be. I said to let me know if you needed anything, and I meant it.'

Now that the bat episode was behind us, my adrenaline plummeted. I rubbed at my temples, suddenly realizing how crappy I felt.

Cohen stepped in closer toward me. 'Are you okay?'

'Too much wine earlier. I'm fine.' I waved him off.

He headed into the kitchen and returned a second later with a glass of water and two white pills. He dropped them in my palm. 'Here. Pain reliever for your headache.'

'Thanks.' I took the pills obediently and finished the glass of water before handing it back to him. It was room temperature and tasted like it had come straight from the tap, but I wasn't about to complain. It was a nice gesture. I'd never talked to my neighbors much, and it was nice to think that someone I could count on lived above me.

I noticed a university sweatshirt hanging from the back of a chair and nodded to it. 'You go to school here too?' DePaul was just down the street, so I guess I shouldn't have been surprised, but this really wasn't a student housing area.

'Yeah. I'm a junior. You?'

'I'm in the second year of my Ph.D.'

'Wow.' He stared at me as though seeing me for the first time. I could practically see him trying to calculate my age. I knew I looked younger than my twenty-five years, and telling people you were studying for a Ph.D. had a way of intimidating them. But Cohen didn't seem thrown off, just...impressed and curious. I liked his honest reaction. According to his grade, he was probably twenty or twenty-one.

I wondered what to do now. There was a bat loose in my apartment, and it was too early—or too late, depending on how you looked at it—to call my landlord.

Cohen stood silently studying me, and I was suddenly self-conscious about my appearance. I'd fallen asleep without washing off my makeup, so I was sure to have smears under my eyes, and my hair probably looked like it'd been styled by a raccoon. Way to make a great second impression.

'Liz? As in Elizabeth?' he asked, softly.

'Nope, Liz as in Eliza. But everyone calls me Liz.'

'Eliza,' he said thoughtfully. The word rolled off his tongue in a way that was both foreign and reminiscent of long ago.

It reminded me of the past too much, and a pain stabbed at my chest. 'Call me Liz,' I corrected.

Cohen was silent for a moment longer, then took my hand and pulled me toward the door. 'Come on, Easy E. Let's go get your hangover fixed up.'

Easy E? 'Where are we going?'

'Breakfast. And don't argue. Bat hunting makes me hungry.' He grabbed a long-sleeved T-shirt and yanked it on over his head.

I laughed and followed him to the door.

I noticed him attach something to his belt loop and when I got closer, I saw that it was a pager.

I followed him down the stairs and fell in line beside him as we began walking down the block. I made a point of eyeing the pager strapped to his waist, cocking an eyebrow at him in question. 'Nineteen-ninety-six called and wants its pager back.'

He chuckled low under his breath, shaking his head. 'I need it for work.' He adjusted his T-shirt so that the obtrusive object was concealed.

'Are you a pimp?'

'Nope.' He smiled.

'A drug dealer?'

'Um, no. I'm a volunteer at the Chicago Fire Department.'

'You're a firefighter?'

'Yeah.'

Wow. That would explain his insanely muscular body. 'How often do you...'

'Get a call?'

I nodded.

'I'm always on call, and attend a training every Monday night for two hours.'

That was interesting. I'd never known a volunteer firefighter. I wondered if that was a lot to manage with school and studying.

We reached a small diner at the corner. Despite living nearby for two years, I'd never been to this place. It always looked a little too shady. A flickering neon sign announced that it was open twenty-four, seven, and bells above the door chimed when Cohen pulled it open and held it for me. Walking by him, I got a lovely whiff of fabric softener and what had to be his own masculine scent. Mmm. I wanted to stop and press my nose into his chest, but I kept walking. The sign said to seat yourself and I chose a pleather booth near the window.

Cohen slid in across from me. He lifted the two menus from the napkin holder and handed me one.

'Thanks.'

'Are you hungry?' he asked.

'Sure. I can eat.' I could always eat. I wasn't one of those girls who pretended not to eat. I liked food, so kill me. And I think if you really asked them, most guys liked a few soft curves on a woman's body. Besides, wine and chocolate hadn't been the most filling of dinners.

'The pancakes here are awesome.' He folded his menu and stuck it back in its place.

'Okay then.' I smiled and handed him my menu too, and he placed it neatly beside his.

The waitress sauntered over with a sweet smile for Cohen. He ordered two stacks of pancakes and after pausing to ask me if I'd like coffee too, he ordered us both a coffee as well.

He was adorable, and even having only just met, I somehow felt totally comfortable around him.

Cohen's gaze drifted from my face to my chest, and he suddenly shifted in his seat and tuned to face the window, his expression uncomfortable. Had I done something wrong?

I looked down and for the first time, remembered my braless state. Crap! The air conditioning had turned my girls into brazen hussies begging for attention. This tank top wasn't exactly full coverage either. I adjusted the shirt as best I could and caught Cohen's reflection in the glass. A smile tugged at his lips.

The waitress delivered two mugs of steaming black coffee to our table.

'Cold?' He smiled slightly, sliding my coffee towards me.

'Shush,' I warned, accepting the coffee and dumped a heap of sugar into the mug, stirring it with more force than was necessary.

'Here.' Cohen pulled his long sleeve T-shirt over his head, leaving him in just his T-shirt, and he held it out to me across the table.

'Thanks.' I shrugged it on. It was still warm and smelled like boy. Delicious boy. Boy that had already turned me down once today. Or was that yesterday now? Not that it mattered. I wouldn't be throwing myself at him again. Period.

I rolled up the sleeves of Cohen's shirt and tried to avoid inhaling the scent of it.

The waitress was soon back with our pancakes, and left a plate in front of each of us. The pancakes were as big as dinner plates and stacked several high. A scoop of butter melted in the center and the scent of warm vanilla wafted in the air.

'Wow. This is bigger than I expected.'

Cohen slid the syrup toward me. 'Think you can handle it?' His smirk was naughty, playful.

Ugh. Why did he have to be so hot?

'Oh, I can handle it like a Goddamn champ.' I cringed. What was I even saying?

Cohen chuckled and scooped the heap of butter off his pancakes and onto the saucer beside his plate. I guess you didn't get a body like that from eating globs of butter.

I had no such worries. And I freaking loved butter. I used my knife to smear the melted puddle all over mine.

'You have a girlfriend?' I asked after swallowing a delicious bite of melt-in-your-mouth pancake.

He nodded, taking another bite. 'I've sort of been seeing someone.'

'But she wasn't over tonight?'

'She doesn't stay over,' he commented, wiping his mouth.

That was curious. Was he the kind of guy that refused to allow a girl to sleep over? Hm. Cohen seemed to provoke more questions than answers.

'What about you? Boyfriend?'

'Nope,' I said, a little too proudly.

He chuckled. 'I have a feeling there's a story there.'

I shrugged. 'Not much to tell, I'm just not looking for a relationship. Besides, once I get my doctorate in another year or two, I'll probably be moving on. I want to have fun and not take things too seriously.'

'Hm.' Cohen looked down, fumbling with his napkin. Had I said something to upset him?

I focused on my breakfast, or whatever meal you called this, given that it was three in the morning.

I realized Cohen had set down his fork and was watching me eat. 'What are you studying?'

'Psychology,' I answered, my tongue darting out to lick a drop of syrup from my bottom lip. 'What about you?'

His eyes followed the movement of my tongue, and he swallowed roughly before answering. 'Business. I figure its generic enough that I'll be able to get a job doing almost anything.'

I nodded. I continued nibbling on my breakfast, while Cohen talked. I learned that he went to school part time and worked as a bouncer at bar downtown in addition to being a volunteer firefighter.

After breakfast, Cohen walked me to my door and stood with me on the covered porch. The moonlight and chirp of crickets in the night air had a dreamy, calming feeling about it.

We stood facing each other. The shadows turned him into an even more handsome creature than before, if that was even possible. He was tall and lean, not an ounce of fat on his body. Square jaw, full mouth, gorgeous blue eyes and short hair.

Cohen hesitated at my front door.

'Thanks for breakfast,' I murmured.

He nodded. 'Anytime.'

I stripped myself of his oversized long-sleeved shirt and handed it back to him. His eyes wandered south to my chest for the briefest of seconds, but enough for me to register he liked what he saw. What can I say? I was blessed in the boob department. Full C's, yet still perky. And currently sporting hard nips again. Damn. This time it had nothing to do with the chill in the air and everything to do with the look on Cohen's face. He was a boob man. It was clear as day.

He cleared his throat. 'Will you be okay?'

Oh yeah. There was a fucking bat in my apartment. This wasn't a date. It was a pity-outing with a neighbor. That was all. Damn. Delusional much, Liz?

I shook my head. 'Well, I'm not sleeping in there.' No way, nuh-uh. 'I'll just have to wait a few more hours until I can call the landlord to come over.'

Cohen frowned. 'What are you going to do in the meantime? It's...' He glanced at his watch. '...way too fucking early.'

I laughed. 'I'm a big girl. I'll be fine. Thanks again.'

I turned for my door, but Cohen grabbed my wrist. 'Come on. You're coming upstairs with me.'

'I am?'

He pressed his other hand into my lower back and guided me to the staircase. 'Up you go.'

I blanched at his presumptuous behavior, yet obediently started up the stairs, relieved that I wouldn't have to wait alone.

When we reached the top, Cohen unlocked the door and pushed it open for me to enter. His apartment was tiny compared to mine. Now that I wasn't all frazzled from the bat incident, I noticed how quaint it was. The pitched ceilings were architecturally interesting, but made it too low for him to comfortably walk in certain spots of the room. The floors were wooden and creaky. I was surprised I'd never heard him walking above me before. He tossed the shirt he'd given me on the back of the sofa.

'Are you tired?'

I shrugged. 'Might as well try to sleep, otherwise I'll be a real bitch tomorrow.'

He laughed. 'You're honest. I like that.'

'Thanks?' I wasn't sure, but that sounded like a compliment. I looked around at the tiny apartment wondering where I'd sleep. 'Won't your girlfriend be mad if I'm sleeping over?'

He shrugged. 'I'm not worried about it.'

I bit my lip to avoid smiling.

He disappeared into his bedroom and I wondered if I was supposed to follow, but before I could decide, he returned with a bundle of blankets and pillows in his arms. He dumped them unceremoniously on the couch. 'You can take my room. I'll sleep out here.'

I surveyed the length of him. 'And how tall are you?'

'Six-two. Why?'

I made a *tsking* sound. 'Yeah, that's what I thought. You will not be sleeping on this couch.' There's no way he would comfortably fit.

He laughed softly. 'I'll be fine.'

'Nonsense. Go to bed. I've got this.' I began unfolding the blankets and arranging them on the couch.

His hands found mine, and he stopped me. 'You're the guest. You should take my bed.' His voice was solemn, sweet.

I couldn't resist placing my hand on his chest. Yep, just as solid and warm as I expected. 'I'm not a guest, sweetheart, I'm an annoying neighbor with a bat problem who woke you up in the middle of the night.'

He smirked.

'Now go to bed.' I patted his chest.

He held me in his gaze. 'You're a feisty little thing, aren't you?'

'Damn straight.'

He laughed out loud. 'And how do you know I'm not a serial killer?'

'Yes, because serial killers usually wear oven mitts for intimidation and buy their victims pancakes before tucking them into bed.' I rolled my eyes for effect.

His mouth twitched in amusement. 'Valid point.' He turned to head to his room. 'Just let me know if you need anything—or if you spot any bats. I've got the oven mitts ready.'

A noise from the other room caught our attention. Cohen's face registered recognition.

He shook his head with a smirk on his face. 'There's just one problem.'

I waited, unsure where this was heading. Maybe his girlfriend had decided to come over after all.

'Bob usually sleeps here.'

Before I had the chance to ask who Bob was, a dog the size of a bear came barreling down the hallway, headed straight for me.

I let out a gasp while Cohen laughed and steered the dog away, stopping him from mauling me. He held the dog's wiggling body in place and scratched behind his ears. The dog's tail walloped against my thigh.

'He tries to sleep in my bed, but I don't usually let him. He's a cover hog.' Cohen smiled.

'What the hell is he?' I took a step back so I was out of the firing line of his tail. He was an enormous fluff ball of curly apricot-colored fur.

'A Labradoodle. Non-shedding.'

'Oh.' *A what-a-doodle?*

Bob leapt onto the couch and flopped himself down onto the blankets I'd just arranged, lying with his head against the armrest as he got into a comfortable position.

Cohen chuckled at the sight of him. 'Unless you're a real dog lover and wouldn't mind cuddling up with this guy, I suggest you come to my room.'

I had no desire to sleep on a couch that doubled as a dog bed, and nodded my consent.

Cohen led the way to his bedroom. It was large and tidy, with king-sized bed in the center. The roof pitched steeply on each side, giving it an intimate feel. He had one small chest of drawers and a single night table that held some loose change and an alarm clock.

His bed was unmade with charcoal gray sheets and a fluffy white down comforter. It looked very inviting.

Cohen studied me for a second. 'Do you...need anything to wear?' He looked down at my jeans.

'Oh. No thanks.' I remembered I had on my sleeping shorts underneath the jeans, and began removing them.

Cohen dropped his eyes, seemingly uncomfortable with watching me undress. I folded my jeans neatly and laid them on the floor beside the bed. I started to crawl into the bed when Cohen's hand on my elbow stopped me.

'The other side, sweetheart.'

Oh. I scooted over to the other side of the bed, nearest the wall.

He yanked his T-shirt off over his head and stripped down to his black boxer briefs. I caught a glimpse of his smooth, tanned skin, just before he crawled in next to me and covered himself with the sheet.

I sensed something had changed between us; the air felt thick and heavy. 'Sorry, I didn't know I was taking your side,' I whispered in the darkness.

'It's okay. I'd prefer to sleep closest to the door. That way if anyone breaks in they have to get through me first.'

Aw. It was a strange notion, but I liked his protective instincts. He was a sweet guy. I didn't usually hang out with many of those. Maybe it had to do with him being a firefighter.

I rolled over on my side and pulled the comforter securely around me, settling in for the night.

Chapter 3

The next morning Cohen stood guard while I dashed inside my apartment to grab a change of clothes and my laptop. We didn't see the bat, but I was glad to have him with me just the same.

He didn't have class until later, so I thanked him for the previous night, and he headed back upstairs to make coffee, while I began the twenty-minute walk to campus.

Despite only getting a few hours of sleep and overindulging on wine, I felt more well-rested than I usually did. Cohen's bed was ridiculously comfortable. And I felt safe with him there. I was used to living alone, but that didn't mean that occasionally I wasn't woken in the night by an unknown noise and was unable to get back to sleep. And was he an absolute gentleman—staying on his own side and pretty much ignoring me completely. I'd slept like a baby in Cohen's bed. Which was strange, since I made it a point not to stay over with guys I slept with. I might fall asleep after sex, but I'd always wake in the middle of the night and slip out of bed unnoticed. Maybe that was why I'd been comfortable staying with Cohen, because we hadn't been intimate. I shrugged the thought away.

I spent the entire day working in the library on my research paper, only stopping for coffee refills and to grab a sandwich from a deli across the street. By six o'clock I was hungry again and in need of a long, hot soak in my jetted tub.

I secured my laptop bag across my chest and set off for the walk home. I checked my phone for messages again, hoping to have an update from my landlord about the bat situation. I was scrolling through text messages when I collided against something solid. I let out a groan and quickly looked up to see who—or what—I'd run into.

It was Cohen. He was out for a run with that damn dog. Bob. It was panting loudly and wagging its tail.

'Hey, Eliza.' Cohen reached out and steadied my shoulders.

'Liz,' I huffed, righting myself.

'Sorry, Bob got excited when he saw you.' Cohen pulled back on the leash, tightening it to hold the dog back from me.

'No—my fault. I was trying to see if I had any messages from our landlord.'

'Oh, he stopped by today. We couldn't find the bat, but we sealed up your chimney flue.'

'We?'

'I didn't have class at the time, so I helped him. You have a really nice place, by the way.'

'Oh, thanks.'

We stared at each other for a few seconds. He looked adorably sexy in his loose-fitting gym shorts and vintage band tee.

'So the bat could still be in there?' I dodged Bob's overeager advance toward me.

Cohen tugged his leash to keep him in line. Bob sat on the ground at our feet. 'Could be. But he probably got out the same way he got in.'

'Okay. Well, thanks. I guess I get to sleep in my own bed tonight.'

'Guess so,' he said. I couldn't help but notice his voice was laced with the slightest bit of disappointment.

When I got home, I did a room-by-room check for the bat, then fed Sugar and Honey Bear who were circling my ankles and meowing eagerly for their dinner. I needed to make myself dinner, but figured a nice hot bath would relax me first. I grabbed a handful of almonds to tide me over and made my way upstairs, munching as I went. I filled the porcelain tub and added my oatmeal lavender bath salts and sank down into the water.

I rested my head against the edge of the tub and breathed in the lavender scent. As the warm water caressed my curves, I couldn't help my mind from wandering to the apartment above mine and a certain off-limits hottie who resided there, seemingly just out of reach.

My few interactions with him had left me curious and wanting more. I wondered about the girlfriend he spoke of, and about his job as a firefighter. Picturing his buff body dressed in a firemen's uniform sent a tingle across my skin, and I closed my eyes, sinking further into the water to enjoy my naughty daydream.

After my bath I felt refreshed, busied myself in the kitchen. I loved to cook, but rarely made anything elaborate for myself.

I gathered armfuls of ingredients from the fridge and cabinets while my mind wandered upstairs to Cohen and wondered if he'd eaten. I could cook for him as a thank you for dealing with the bat and sealing up my chimney flue. But I didn't want to seem too overeager, and I was sure he had better things to do then spend time with me.

I set a pot of water to boil on the stovetop and set the flickering flame to high before dumping in a palmful of sea salt to season the water. I wrestled my seldom-used food processor out from a lower cabinet and added in handfuls of basil leaves and pine nuts, before topping it off with a splash of olive oil and setting it to purée. Once the water was boiling, I dropped in the linguine and set the timer, then popped a frozen loaf of my favorite French bread in the oven to bake.

I'd been unconsciously making enough for two. This was silly; I'd just go up and invite him for dinner.

Halfway up the stairs, I hesitated and stopped. What if his girl-friend was over? Or maybe he already had dinner plans. I didn't want to sound like I was desperate for company. Maybe I could just ask if he had any plans before bringing up the elaborate dinner waiting for us downstairs.

I shook my head, reminding myself that the first step was seeing if he was even home. I continued up the stairs and when I reached his door, I could hear music playing, and knocked loud enough to be sure he could hear me. A second later, the door swung open.

Cohen stood before me in dark fitted jeans and a baby-blue cotton Henley that made his eyes look amazing. 'Easy E!' He pulled me inside. He was holding an acoustic guitar in one hand, and I realized that was where the music had been coming from. 'Want a beer?' He took a sip from a bottle of Red Stripe and before I could respond, Bob came charging down the hall and launched himself through the air with enough force to knock me to the ground. He landed squarely on my chest.

Ompf. A gust of air escaped my lungs at the contact.

'Oh, shit. Bob, get off,' Cohen pulled the dog back from me, but not before he got in a few slobbery kisses.

I wiped my face with my sleeve and took Cohen's outstretched hand.

'Sorry about that. He's bigger than you and he just gets excited.'

I released a sigh and rubbed my aching tailbone. 'It's okay.'

Cohen brushed off my backside and helped to straighten my tank top. His fingers brushed against my waist, and the heat of his hands through my top caused my heart to thump in my chest. Bob's indiscretion was forgiven and the only thing I could concentrate on now was Cohen and how amazing his deep-blue eyes looked, highlighted by his baby-blue shirt.

As if realizing his hands were still against my waist, Cohen dropped them and stepped back. 'How about that beer?'

'Actually I was wondering if you had plans tonight.'

He took another swig. 'Not unless you count drinking alone and messing around on my guitar.'

I smiled. 'Well I was cooking dinner downstairs and made enough for two. I thought I'd invite you over as a thank you for all that bat business.'

'Sounds great.'

He returned his guitar to its stand in the corner, ducking from the pitched ceiling as he did so. He patted Bob's head then followed me downstairs with the bottle of beer still dangling from his hand.

As soon as we entered my apartment, the vibe felt all wrong, like I was trying too hard. There were candles burning on my fireplace mantle, and soft jazz music playing in the background. God, was I old or what? I needed to remember that he was a college kid, more likely to listen to the latest indie band or hip hop sensation. I contemplated blowing out the candles and changing the music, but instead decided to shrug it off. I didn't want to call more attention to it, and Cohen didn't seem to mind in the least, wandering ahead of me through the apartment.

I crossed the living room, following Cohen through the rooms I'd meticulously decorated with light earth tones in creams and browns to coordinate with the dark wood floors.

When I turned for the kitchen, Cohen followed dutifully. The kitchen was small but was remodeled before I moved in, and boasted state-of-the-art fixtures and appliances. I cringed when I remembered I'd also lit a few candles on the center granite slab island.

'Smells awesome. What'd you make?'

Of course his mind was on the free meal, not the ambience. *God, get a grip, Liz.*

'Basil pesto pasta with grilled chicken.' I opened the double door fridge and pulled out a bottle of white wine. 'Would you like some?' I held the bottle up for Cohen to inspect.

23

He drained his bottle of beer and set the empty next to the sink. 'Sure. Where do you keep the glasses?'

'Behind you.' I nodded to the mahogany wine cabinet on the far side of the kitchen that held numerous bottles of wine and had racking where the wine glasses were stored.

He retrieved two of the glasses, while I concentrated on uncorking the wine.

Cohen's hands met mine on the bottle of wine and corkscrew. 'Let me.'

I stepped back and allowed him to open the wine, taking the opportunity to watch him uninterrupted. His hands were large, tapering to long, slender fingers with neatly trimmed nails. The backs of his hands were lightly covered in fine blonde hairs I could see when they caught the light. Everything about this man was attractive. From his clean cut features, to his broad shoulders to his flat stomach. Something about the idea of being with him excited me. But I had never felt so unsure before in the presence of a man. He was friendly and polite, but he didn't seem overly interested.

While Cohen poured us each a healthy glass of wine, I pulled the serving dish of pasta from inside the oven, where I'd set it to keep warm. I removed the hot loaf of French bread next, and placed it on the stone block to slice. Cohen helped me move everything over the barstool seating area at the end of the long island. I grabbed the butter and a green salad from the fridge and joined him on a stool.

He removed his pager and set it beside him. 'Hopefully I don't get a call tonight.' It was strange to think that at any moment he could be summoned away, his evening interrupted. 'Cheers.' He clinked his wine glass with mine and we both took a sip. It was my favorite white wine, Santa Margherita Pinot Grigio. It was crisp and refreshing and paired perfectly with the light pasta meal.

I watched Cohen take a bite and chew. He closed his eyes just briefly, savoring the bite of crisp basil pesto and pine nuts, balanced by the heavy cream. 'You're a great cook,' he offered after several more bites.

'Thanks.' I relaxed a little more in my seat and began eating.

We kept up an easy conversation during dinner, pausing to tease each other, or smile and sip our wine. It was nice. Though I enjoyed cooking, I rarely did so for myself. It just seemed like too much of a hassle for one person. I usually ate a bag of microwave popcorn or a bowl of cereal for dinner instead, but it was nice having someone to cook for.

Cohen's pager rattled nosily against the granite island. He picked it up and frowned as he read the message.

'What is it?'

He shook his head. 'I can't go on a call if I've had more than two drinks.'

Oh. 'Is it okay if you miss one?'

He nodded. 'I don't like to, and I have to make it to at least fifty-percent of all calls to stay active, but it should be fine.'

He turned off the pager and went back to eating.

Cohen suddenly dropped his fork against the side of his plate, the clinking sound startling me. 'Are there nuts in this?'

I looked from the pasta to the panicked expression on his face. 'Um, yes, there are pine nuts in the sauce. Why, what's wrong?'

He leapt from his seat, his napkin fluttering to the floor. 'I'm allergic. Where's the bathroom?'

I was too stunned to answer and instead pointed down the hall. Cohen took off jogging in the direction I'd indicated. The first door he opened was a broom closet. I quickly followed behind him to steer him into the guest bathroom farther down the hall. He fell to his knees over the toilet bowl and threw up nosily.

Eek. I cringed away from the sound of him coughing and vomiting. I felt terrible. How was I supposed to know he was allergic to pine nuts?

Kendall Ryan

Once he was finished, he wiped his mouth with a wad of toilet paper and sank to the floor and sat with his back against the wall. I reached over and flushed the toilet. Cohen's eyes met mine and he groaned. I don't think he'd realized I was still in the room with him. His skin was pale and he was covered in a thin sheen of sweat.

'Are you okay?'

He nodded. 'I think so.' He closed his eyes and let his head fall back against the wall. I took a washcloth from the basket near the sink and wet it with cold water. I wrung it out and knelt down near Cohen. I pressed the cool washcloth to his forehead.

He briefly opened his eyes. 'Thanks,' he croaked.

'I feel terrible, Cohen. I didn't mean...'

'You didn't know. It's okay. I should've asked, but I didn't see any nuts.' He closed his eyes again and relaxed against the wall while I continued to dab the cool cloth against his flushed skin. He really was beautiful. I'd never recalled thinking of a man as beautiful before, but Cohen truly was.

He opened his eyes and studied me. I realized I'd stopped moving the cloth and was just staring at him. 'What?' he asked.

'Nothing.' I moved the cloth to the back of his neck.

He dropped his head between his knees, giving me better access. 'That feels nice.'

A pain sprang through my chest and I stood abruptly, suddenly needing some space away from this tender moment.

Cohen stood a minute later. 'Sorry I ruined dinner.'

'Are you kidding? You do not need to apologize. I could have killed you.'

He chuckled. 'I'm not deathly allergic. I just get really sick. Seriously, I'm fine now. And it tasted really good.'

'Before you threw it up?' I said wryly.

'Exactly.' He smiled.

26

I rolled my eyes. *Boys*. 'Do you want to go lie down?'

'Ah, sure. If you'll come with me.' He grinned. 'We can watch a movie.'

'Sounds good.'

After we quickly cleaned up the kitchen, Cohen led the way back upstairs to his apartment where Bob was eagerly awaiting our return. Cohen kept him from mauling me, and I made a halfhearted attempt at petting him, but it was so obvious I wasn't a dog person, Cohen just laughed and told Bob to go lie down. Bob flopped himself unceremoniously onto the wood floor and laid his head on his paws.

I looked around the living room for the first time noticing there was no TV. Before I could question how we were going to watch a movie, Cohen led the way to his bedroom.

There was a large flat screen television mounted on his wall across from the bed. 'This okay?' Cohen held up the DVD case for a romantic comedy I hadn't yet seen.

I stifled my surprise that he owned the movie, and nodded instead. 'Sure.'

'Okay, pop it in. I'm going to go brush my teeth.'

He tossed me the case and I caught it easily. 'I'm on it.'

I put the DVD in and settled on his bed and began watching the previews. I scooted over to my side, the side of the bed farthest from the door, remembering his notion that he'd protect me if anyone broke in. I scolded myself thinking a side of his bed was mine.

Just when I was starting to wonder what was taking him so long, I heard the sound of water running and a shower curtain being pulled back. Dirty thoughts flashed through my mind. Was that an open invitation to join him in the shower? Other than the odd lingering glance, Cohen hadn't indicated he wanted to be anything more than friends. I had never really had a close guy friend, so this was sort of new territory for me, but I liked it.

A few minutes later, just as the previews were wrapping up, Cohen came back in the room, dressed in a pair of loose-fitting gym shorts and a white V-neck T-shirt. He settled onto the bed next to me, folding the pillow in half under his head and punching it into place. 'Sorry, I decided to take a shower too.'

'No problem.' I looked over at him and smiled. His tan skin was delicious against the white cotton shirt. And he smelled like crisp, clean soap and a hint of spicy cologne.

I shifted closer and breathed him in.

'What?' He smirked.

'You smell good.'

'I do?'

I nodded. 'Like soap...and...' I leaned in again to try and identify it.

He smiled. 'Come here.' He held out his arm until I scooted against his side. He was warm and the firm muscles of his body felt amazing pressed against mine. It was times like this I couldn't decipher his motivations.

The movie started but I was too distracted to concentrate on it, instead noticing Cohen's bare feet which were long and tan, with fine light hair sprinkled on the top. Why had I never noticed before how sexy a man's bare feet could be?

Cohen absently traced a slow pattern on the inside of my forearm, dragging his thumbnail down to my palm, and back up over the inside of my wrist. I wondered if he could feel my pulse jump at the simple touches, if he realized the effect he was having on me. I snuck a glance up at his face, and he seemed to be oblivious, absorbed into the movie. Despite my body's urgings I didn't want to be the aggressor with Cohen. I may have had no problem in the past taking what I wanted, but I wanted him to choose me. And I wouldn't do anything to interfere, as much as I might be tempted to.

I swallowed and lay completely immobile, waiting for his hand to make a more daring move, but he continued right on skimming his fingertips softly along my skin, seemingly unaware of the fact that he was turning me on. I decided upon conducting an experiment to see what kind of response I could provoke from him. I placed my hand flat on his stomach and waited for several minutes for him to get used to the contact. Then, I let my fingertips drift along his washboard abs, slowly gliding over his ribs, and then back down, stopping just above the waistband of his shorts. His hand stilled on my skin, resting at my pulse point and I knew he could feel its insistent thrumming.

He lifted up on his elbow to look down at me. I knew I was flushed and pink like I'd been caught with my hand in the cookie jar. He placed a hand against my cheek, as if checking my temperature.

'You're warm. Are you feeling okay?' His eyes met mine, narrowing with confusion and worry.

No I'm not okay, I'm horny as hell and you're driving me crazy!
'Fine, why?'

He shook his head, like he was clearing a thought. 'Okay. I'll just get you some water.' He stood from the bed and crossed the room.

I don't want any damn water, I want some cock! I fell back onto the pillow with a huff. This boy was going to be the death of me.

When Cohen returned with the water, I dutifully swallowed the big gulp he insisted I have before he would join me on the bed again.

Once that was done, he nestled me in against his body and placed his arm around me, his fingertips absently skimming along my shoulder. My skin tingled all over. I was hyperaware of each tiny movement of his fingers, wanting him to touch me elsewhere, to explore more of my body. But this time when he picked up my hand once again and began rubbing my knuckles with his thumb, I tried not to read anything into it.

'Enjoying the movie?' he whispered.

'Mm-hmm.' I didn't trust myself enough to form actual coherent words just then. The room around us had grown dark except for the faint glow of the TV, and the air buzzed with sexual attraction.

He turned my hand over and held it in his, continuing to massage my palms with the pad of his thumb. It was simple and innocent, yet completely fucking turning me on.

Cohen held my palm up and looked at it. 'Your hands are tiny.'

My breathing turned shallow and I waited in anticipation for what was building between us, hoping it would advance beyond the just-friends stage.

'This is your life line.' He traced his thumb along the center of my palm, sending a ticklish rush through me. He brought my hand closer to inspect it in the dim light. 'And your love line. But it stops abruptly right here.' He tapped near my thumb.

I let out the breath I'd been holding. 'Yeah, I swore off the whole commitment thing years ago.'

'Bad experience?' He set my hand down between us.

'Something like that.'

'Want to talk about it?'

'Not really.' I never talked about *him*. Ever. Not even with Ashlyn. Cohen smiled at me sadly, like I was broken. I didn't want him to feel pity for me. I didn't want him to feel anything for me, except maybe desire. That wouldn't be so bad. He picked up my hand again and laced his fingers with mine.

'I'm here if you want to talk.'

'Thanks.' I gave his hand a squeeze. Against my will, I found my mind wandering to my parents' brutal divorce a few years ago, which was the other part of the story. The part I was more comfortable allowing myself to remember. 'My parents had the catastrophe of all divorces during my freshman year of college. They don't speak at all anymore.'

'Is that the reason you're a commitment-phobe?'

'It's part of the reason.' *A small part.* 'What about you? Are your parents still married?'

'I never knew my dad. He took off on my mom when she was pregnant with me. She was only eighteen.'

'Wow. That must have been hard.'

'Yeah, but we managed.' His jaw flexed, and I backed off, sensing he didn't want to answer questions about his past any more than I did.

Cohen continued to hold my hand throughout the movie and I rested my head on his chest, content with the silence between us.

When the movie ended, he turned it off while I stretched out on his bed.

He looked down at me and smiled. 'Tired?'

I nodded.

'I've got to take Bob out. I can walk you home, or…'

'Or?' My eyebrow quirked up.

'You could sleep over again.'

I grinned up at him despite my best attempt to act cool and unaffected. 'You like having me in your bed, rather than Bob?'

He laughed. 'Hell yeah, Easy E. You smell a lot better too.' He leaned down and sniffed my hair. 'Yep. Like flowers and sunshine.'

'Your bed is insanely comfortable. Let me just go down and get pajamas while you're walking Bob.'

'Cool.' He smiled, seemingly happy.

We headed downstairs, and while Cohen took a stroll around the block, I dashed inside and brushed my teeth, set the dishwasher to run overnight and then picked out the perfect pajamas to tempt Cohen.

A teeny tiny pair of hot-pink shorts with the word SEXY written across the butt and a white tank top that had been washed so many times it had shrunk to fit snugly, the thin cotton hugging my breasts. Lastly, I stripped off my bra and hoisted the girls on display to show a little cleavage. There was no way Cohen wouldn't notice these beauties. I giggled to myself and headed back outside.

Chapter 4

Cohen was waiting on my front porch to escort me back upstairs, Bob sitting by his side. Something tugged inside me. I liked that he'd waited rather than heading back upstairs without me. I'd started to feel slightly ridiculous about this slumber party, but when I saw him waiting patiently for me, all doubts were pushed from my mind. He wanted me to stay over just as much as I did. I couldn't explain it, but maybe that was okay.

'Ready?' I locked my front door then turned to face him.

His eyes started at my face then travelled south, stopping at my chest. His lips parted just slightly and he inhaled a shaky breath. 'Uh…yeah.' He ushered me against his side. 'Cold?' He rubbed the length of my arm, unaware that my goose bumps had nothing to do with the chill in the air and everything to do with the desire I saw reflected in his eyes.

I was about to mutter something cute about him keeping me warm, when Bob chose that exact moment to stick his snout in the crotch of my shorts. Cohen chuckled and redirected the dogs face from between my legs.

Sheesh. Did I mention I hated dogs?

When we made it inside, Cohen got Bob settled for the night on the sofa, then directed me to his room. He waited for me to walk in ahead of him, and I couldn't help giving my hips a little

32

extra swing as I moved. Wearing those shorts out in public was probably illegal, considering the amount of leg—and even curve of butt cheek—that was peeking out from underneath.

I crawled onto the bed, my bottom hoisted up in the air on display. But when I got to my side of the mattress, and looked for Cohen's reaction, he turned away quickly, and busied himself on the other side of his room, removing his jeans and folding them on top of the dresser.

I tugged the covers up around me.

We settled into bed, and Cohen rolled over to face me. 'Is this weird—you staying here?'

I shook my head. 'Not if we're okay with it.'

He nodded.

Without realizing it, my hand had wandered onto his stomach. He shifted under my palm and inhaled sharply. I looked up and met his eyes. They were inquisitive and locked on mine. And even in the darkness of his bedroom, I could see his curiosity at what might happen next.

His hand came to rest at the base of my throat. It was heavy and warm. He lightly brushed his fingertips along my bare collarbone, tracing a lazy pattern on my skin. The roughness of his fingers against that soft, innocent patch of flesh set my heart racing. I wanted more.

I licked my lips, waiting. He bent his head down to mine, while at the same time burying his hand in my hair. He lightly kissed the corner of my jaw. 'God you're beautiful,' he murmured.

I swallowed roughly at his declaration. He was so open and honest. I didn't want or need touching and romantic, but every caress, every gaze from Cohen felt like more. This was nothing like being with Stu and that scared the shit out of me.

I pressed my hand against his stomach, forcing him flat to the bed, then moved on top of him, one of my thighs on each side of his. He looked up at me, full of curiosity and desire. I leaned down and kissed his lips. His tongue found its way into my mouth and I pressed my hips into his while our tongues mingled and flirted. He was the perfect kisser. Not too timid, but not overeager either. His hand came up to cup my jaw and he tilted my head, finding the right angle to deepen the kiss. A wave of desire for him shot straight between my legs. I let out a ragged groan and Cohen placed his hands on my shoulders, applying pressure to break the kiss. I leaned back slightly and met his eyes. 'Holy hell,' I muttered.

He chuckled. 'Yeah.' His head fell back against the pillow and he closed his eyes. 'I don't know if this is such a good idea, Eliza.'

I bristled at his use of my full name. 'Because you're seeing someone?'

He opened his eyes again and looked at me. 'Actually, no. We only went out a few times, and I haven't talked to her since I met you.'

Since he met me? 'Oh. Then…?' *What's the problem?* I added silently.

His hands moved from my shoulders to my waist and he tugged me in a little tighter toward him. I took it as a sign and angled my mouth to meet his, then waited.

Cohen's lips brushed against mine, barely touching, his warm breath mingling with my own. It was incredibly hot and made me anxious for more. 'I know I shouldn't, but God I want you.'

Without further protests or explanations we continued kissing for several minutes. I found myself on my back with Cohen hovering above me, kissing and nibbling on my collarbone, jaw, and neck. I rocked my hips against him, eager for more contact. I forgot this kind of foreplay existed. My appointments with Stu were usually straight to the point, insert object A into object B. And most other guys I'd been with were the same way.

'Fuck, you feel good,' I murmured in between short breaths.

I felt him smile against my skin.

I was two seconds away from begging him to fuck me when he suddenly stopped and pulled back to look at me. 'You. Are. Trouble.' He peppered my lips with kisses, punctuating each word.

I couldn't help but grin. It'd been a long time since I'd been told I was trouble. Guys typically appreciated that I was an instigator. Sensing that Cohen wanted to stop, I scooted out from under him and up toward the headboard until I was half sitting. He sat next to me, propped up in the same way, trying to get his breathing under control.

I felt dizzy and confused. I tried not to frown and adjusted my shirt, which had ridden up to expose my belly. Cohen's eyes flashed hungrily at my skin, before looking away. I didn't understand what was stopping Cohen from wanting more with me. Was I not his type?

'Are you okay?' Cohen asked.

I nodded, not trusting my voice.

He ran his fingers through his hair and closed his eyes. When he opened them, he took my hand and turned to face me. 'Look, I'm sorry, okay? I know you're not looking for a relationship.'

I sensed he was trying to find the right words, but it was also something more.

'That doesn't mean we can't have some fun though, right?'

He let out a ragged breath. 'You're toxic to my willpower,' he whispered, as if talking to himself. 'Growing up with a single mom, who was only a teenager when she had me, she drilled into me to never to get a girl pregnant. The way he left her… God.' He ran his hands through his hair. 'I don't know why I'm telling you all this.' He stared up at the ceiling and pulled in another breath. 'I vowed to make something of myself. I've been working full time since I was fifteen, became a volunteer firefighter when I was eighteen, and I vowed to never treat a woman the way my mother was treated.'

'Cohen, I don't understand. I'm not worried about getting pregnant, I'm on the pill.'

He swallowed, his Adam's apple bobbing in his throat. 'I...'

'Cohen?' I placed my palm flat on his stomach. 'Tell me.'

'I'm waiting for the girl I love.'

'Waiting?'

'Waiting,' he said firmly.

Oh, fuck. Waiting! I felt like the breath was knocked out of my lungs. A virgin? This good-looking, beautiful man? Was there something wrong with him I was unaware of? Deformed? Small package? *Oh, please don't let him have a small package.*

I pushed away the crazy thoughts swirling inside my head. It was an honorable thing he'd chosen. He clearly loved and respected his mother, and he didn't want to repeat his father's mistakes. But wasn't this a little extreme? I didn't know anyone who'd chosen to remain celibate for so long. Well, except for Ashlyn. She once admitted to me she was a virgin until she was twenty-two.

'Eliza? Say something.'

'Are you waiting for marriage?' I asked.

'No. I'm, just waiting for the right girl, I guess.'

I knew it wasn't an idea I should even entertain, but part of me wondered if I could be the right girl for Cohen, if I would be his first. I pushed the thought away as quickly as it appeared. He and I were interested in two very different things. I couldn't allow myself to get attached to anyone. And Cohen wanted the full package. Love, romance, marriage. He was more traditional in his views, maybe because he grew up without all that. I knew no one could make me happy but me and to not put stock in something that might not last.

He picked up my hand and laced his fingers with mine. 'I just wanted to be up front. Other girls have had strange reactions and gotten pissed...' he tapered off.

36

'They've gotten mad?'

'Yeah. One girl I went out with a few times last year got pissed when I wouldn't and she started screaming at me and left in the middle of the night.'

'Seriously?'

'Yeah.' He traced his finger down the length of my forearm.

Hm. I could see his choice hadn't always been an easy one, but he'd stuck to the decision he made. It was commendable, even if I couldn't understand it. 'Well, thank you for telling me.' I pressed a soft kiss to his cheek. I wasn't sure what this new information meant between us.

He took my face in his hands and brought my mouth to his, pressing a gentle kiss to my lips. 'Goodnight, Eliza.'

'Night.' I laid back and closed my eyes, but there was no way in hell I'd be falling asleep anytime soon with all this new information swirling around inside my brain. Not to mention the weight of Cohen's warm body next to mine and his steady deep breaths were a constant reminder of something I could never have.

Chapter 5

I needed an appointment with Stu the following day. Desperately. Lying all night next to the sexy-but-oh-so-off-limits Cohen had me all worked up.

I showered and dressed at my place after leaving Cohen lying in bed, grabbed a large iced Americano on my way, and arrived a few minutes early for a meeting with my advisor. I used that time to text Stu about meeting up at his office later.

I was on edge all day long and my afternoon appointment with Stu couldn't come fast enough. I knew he couldn't completely satisfy me—not when what I wanted was Cohen—but it was something to take the edge off.

When I arrived at Stu's office, the door was sitting partially open. I knocked lightly and peeked inside.

Stu was talking to a student. I was about to duck back out and allow them to finish, when the student turned to face me. It was Cohen.

'Eliza?' Cohen's expression was one of confusion. 'How'd you know I was here? Everything okay?'

I swallowed roughly, like a kid caught with her hand in the cookie jar. 'I'm here to meet with Stu— Um, Professor Gibson, actually.'

'You two know each other?' Cohen asked, looking between Stu and I.

'Yeah.' I offered no explanation and Stu stayed silent as well.

'And how do you two know each other?' Stu inquired a tense moment later.

'We're neighbors,' I said.

Cohen looked suspiciously between me and Stu.

'Okay, well, thanks for the extension on the midterm paper,' Cohen said, standing and picking up his bag.

'No problem. Just let me know anytime your volunteering interferes with your studies. I think it's admirable what you're doing.'

Cohen stood facing me and smiled. 'See you at home tonight?' He smiled.

'Of course,' I whispered, breathless.

Then he was gone and Stu was staring at me wearily. Seeing Cohen here had unnerved me. Now it felt wrong to be doing whatever it was I was doing with Stu. If I closed the door now and continued on with what I'd originally come to do, Cohen could be lurking outside and I just couldn't do that to him.

'Sorry Stu, something came up and I'm not going to be able to keep our appointment.'

'Does this have anything to do with your *neighbor*?' The word dripped with innuendo.

'Something like that.' I released a deep sigh and headed back out into the hall. Cohen was nowhere in sight.

Since it looked like sexual relief wasn't on the agenda today, I texted Ashlyn. I needed some girl time. Stat.

We met up a short while later for happy hour at a small pub halfway between her new apartment and my townhouse. She and Aiden had bought a place together, wanting to start over fresh. It was a beautiful loft with modern touches. It was half Ashlyn, with mismatched furniture and bright colors and half Aiden, with classy paintings hung on the walls. I'd been over there a handful of times to visit and to see Thomas, their cat who I'd fostered for a little while. Owning three cats was practically announcing to the world that I was an aspiring cat lady, which I was—but still. That was my business.

I had already ordered a glass of Shiraz when Ashlyn came bounding through the door, her hair spinning around her face as the wind caught it. I waved and she started toward me.

She hopped up onto the stool next to me and smiled. I could read her like a book. 'You just had sex, didn't you?'

She blushed wickedly. 'No comment.'

I signaled the bartender and ordered a glass of Bordeaux for Ashlyn, knowing it was her favorite. 'Thanks.' She grinned and accepted the glass, bringing it to her lips. 'So what's up? Your text made it sound like there was some type of emergency.'

'Yeah, sorry about that. It's nothing really, just guy trouble.'

She took another sip. 'With you, guy trouble is never *nothing*. Now spill.'

I chuckled, knowing she was right. 'You know how I've been sleeping with Stu?'

She nodded, and rolled her eyes. I knew she didn't approve.

'Well, now this little hottie moved in upstairs and I've spent the last two nights with him.'

'Dang, girl.'

Ashlyn never judged me or made me feel bad about my behavior with men, but she did try to poke and prod me into a normal, healthy relationship whenever she got the chance.

I swirled the wine in my glass. 'Sleeping. Not fucking.'

She pursed her lips. 'That doesn't sound like you.'

'I know. He's a volunteer firefighter, a junior in undergrad, a good boy, yet sexy as hell. Visits his momma every Sunday.'

'Wow, a volunteer firefighter? How much can one girl take? Does he rescue puppies too?' she joked.

I chuckled. Knowing Cohen, he probably did. He seemed to be an animal lover. 'Here's real the kicker—he's a virgin, waiting for the right girl.'

Ashlyn choked on her last sip of wine and broke into a coughing fit. I glanced around the bar, and all eyes were turned our way at the commotion. I patted her back and she lifted one hand. 'Sorry, wrong pipe,' she croaked.

'Get together, girl.' I swatted her backside playfully, and she shot me a look.

'Don't spring that kind of shit on me, mid-swallow. You. And a sexy, innocent virgin? Oh, hell, no.'

I laughed and took another healthy sip of my own wine, finding my stomach currently doing somersaults, and needing something to distract me. Was hanging around Cohen as bad of an idea as Ashlyn made it seem? No, I didn't think so. We were both adults. We could choose what we did and didn't want to do. It wasn't like I was going to purposely tempt him into sleeping with me. *Much.*

'I've got it under control, Ash.'

'So you guys are…friends?' she scoffed, clearly suspicious.

'Yeah. Friends.'

She let out a hearty laugh. 'Okay then. Let me know how that works out for you.' She continued shaking her head, trying to contain her laugh as her expression turned more serious. 'Gosh, Liz, you're more jacked up than I give you credit for sometimes.'

I narrowed my eyes. 'What's that supposed to mean?'

'You choose men that are so unavailable to you. It's almost comical how you find yourself in these situations. I'd just like to see you have a normal relationship at some point.'

'You know I'm not looking for that.'

'I know you're not. But I reserve hope that someday maybe you'll grow out of this.' She waved her hand in my general direction.

A few minutes later Ashlyn's hand on my forearm snapped my attention back to her. I don't know how long I'd been silently staring off into space.

'You can't give up on having a real, meaningful relationship just because there are a few jerks out there.'

I gave her a pointed stare. 'I do have meaningful relationships. There's you,' I counted off on my fingers, 'my cats, and my vibrator.'

She shook her head. 'I meant something with a penis.'

I avoided mentioning my flesh rocket in the night table by my bed, and instead pressed my lips into a line, sure that Ashlyn would only add on the stipulation that the penis be attached to a living, breathing male. *Pfft. Overrated.* I'd been taking care of myself, including all my needs, for several years now. There was no reason to mess with the system. I firmly stood by the saying *If it ain't broke, don't fix it.*

I fiddled with the stem of my wine glass. 'Enough about my non-existent love life. Tell me what's new with you.'

She patted my knee. 'You know I love you, sweetie. As long as you're happy, I'm happy.'

'I'm happy.' I plastered on a smile, hoping she wouldn't notice the way my mouth twitched at the corners. The truth was I hadn't been happy in a long time. Five years to be exact. That was when after one fateful night, I fought to turn off all emotion. And I intended to keep it that way.

Seemingly unaware of the personal battle raging inside me, Ashlyn continued. 'Aiden rented a lake house for next weekend on Lake Michigan. There are two bedrooms, so of course you're invited. Sort of a celebration of the end of summer, before the weather turns.'

'Yeah. I'm in. That sounds fun.' Catching some late-summer sun, drinking with Ashlyn, it would be a nice end to the summer before the pain sure to follow in this fall term for us both. I only hoped I didn't feel like too much of a third wheel on their sure-to-be-romantic getaway. I gulped down the remainder of my wine and signaled the bartender for another.

Chapter 6

After Cohen's admission about being a virgin, I found myself inadvertently steering clear of him. I hadn't slept over again, and I hadn't seen Stu either. It was too strange knowing Stu was one of Cohen's professors. Also, I couldn't seem to shake Ashlyn's judgments. I wasn't ready for a relationship, plain and simple, and so I knew deep down that I shouldn't lead Cohen on. He knew what he was looking for—and I wasn't it, so there was no sense in fooling myself.

After my run early that Sunday morning, I saw Cohen and Bob just returning from a run themselves.

I stopped in front of our house to stretch. 'Hey there,' I called as he jogged the last few paces toward me.

'Hey, Easy E.' He smiled.

I couldn't help but chuckle at the ridiculous nickname that seemed to have stuck. Yes, because being named after an old-school rapper was so endearing.

Cohen's smile alone worked to ease some of the tension of my conflicting emotions over the last few days.

He stopped beside me, breathing hard, and Bob dropped to the sidewalk, his tongue lolling from his mouth. 'Where have you been? You haven't been over.'

I looked down at my tennis shoes. 'Sorry. I've been busy.'

He tipped my chin up to meet his eyes. 'You were weirded out by what I told you.'

It wasn't a question, and I didn't respond. I just held his blue gaze, searching for what, I didn't know.

He chuckled. 'Don't get weird on me. I'm still the same guy. Sure, I've probably held myself to stricter standards than some, but don't treat me different now that you know.'

'I'm sorry,' I blurted without thinking, realizing that my apology had just proven he was right—I had been treating him differently.

'Bob and I have missed you.' He reached down and ruffled the dog behind his ear.

'Do you want to grab some breakfast or something?' I offered.

He smiled at me again, but shook his head. 'No, I take my mom and little sister to church Sunday mornings. You're welcome to join us.'

'Church? Me?' *Um, no thanks.*

'Come on, it's probably not as bad as what you're thinking. Come with me, and we'll get breakfast together after—just the two of us.'

I have no idea what possessed me to say yes, but somehow I found myself nodding. I don't know if it was to make up for my obvious dismissal of him after he admitted his deepest secrets, or just because he was impossible to say no to, gazing down at me with those beautiful blue eyes, telling me he'd missed me, but whatever the reason, I found myself showered and dressed and back on my porch to meet him thirty minutes later. Lord, help me.

Cohen strolled down the stairs, dressed in pressed khakis and a button-down shirt. He looked handsome, and even younger somehow. Even his normally messy hair was fashioned into place with some type of styling product. It was hard to take my eyes off him walking towards me, which was why it took me a second to notice that Bob was with him.

'Does Bob go everywhere with you?'

He rolled his eyes. 'My sister Grace got this dog for me when she found out that our fire station dog was killed. Bob was her birthday present to me. But she's really attached to him too, so I bring him to my mom's house whenever I go home.'

'Gotcha.'

We walked to the curb where an antique-looking blue Jeep was parked.

He secured Bob in the back and then came around the side to open my door and help me inside.

He surveyed my most modest knee-length black skirt and burgundy top. 'You clean up nice.'

'Thanks,' I mumbled, climbing into the Jeep.

His mom lived on the south side of Chicago, about a twenty-minute drive, and we kept up an easy conversation on the way.

'How old is your little sister?'

'She's eight. My mom had this boyfriend—a real dirt bag. He stuck around until she was eight months pregnant and then took off.'

He strummed his thumb against the steering wheel, as if lost in thought. 'She was such a wreck that the baby came early. I was fifteen and began working full time to help take care of her, and help out with a newborn. I don't even remember most of my freshman year of high school.'

No wonder he'd chosen to remain celibate. If that wasn't a solid birth control method, I didn't know what was. 'So you've been working since then?'

'Yeah. And when I was eighteen, I enrolled in an EMT and firefighters course so I'd always have something to fall back on.'

'Smart.' I nodded.

'There have been times when it didn't feel so smart—like when rushing into a burning building in the middle of the night , not knowing if I'd make it out again.'

45

'That must have been a crazy way to grow up—so fast and with such responsibility.'

'Sort of. But it was all I knew. I had a choice. I could rebel and go the path of some of my friends—get into drugs, parties and girls—but I knew if I did, that'd make me no better than my own father, or Grace's.'

Cohen's strength and character continued to impress me. I watched him maneuver through the Chicago traffic with ease, smartly navigating the Jeep into the fastest moving lanes and dodging backups like he was quite used to driving these highways. It was impressive to watch. I rarely drove, and being from a small town, the Chicago highway system still scared me.

Soon, we were stopping in front of a tiny brick house with a patchy yellow lawn.

'Home sweet home,' he said, putting the Jeep into park.

Before we were even out of the car, a little girl with messy blonde hair was running through the yard toward us. Cohen unlatched the back of the Jeep, releasing the restraint that held a very excited Labradoodle in place.

'Boo Boo!' she called and Bob happily darted toward her. She fell back onto the lawn under the weight of the dog and giggled while he lapped wet kisses all over her cheeks.

'Boo Boo?' I cocked an eyebrow at Cohen.

'Don't ask. I'm not calling a damn dog Boo Boo. I changed it to Bob.'

Bob continued slobbering all over the little girl for several minutes and I couldn't help but laugh. Eventually, Grace extricated herself from the dog and ran over to stand in front of us, her eyes wide and curious.

'This is my sister…um…' Cohen hesitated, scratching his head. 'What's your name again?'

'Grace!' she shouted, shoving against his stomach with all her might. He didn't even budge.

Her grin couldn't be dampened though and she threw her arms around his waist, hugging him with abandon. I'd grown up with a brother two years older. I didn't recall being that excited to see him. Ever. It was sweet. Cohen leaned down to kiss the top of her head. 'Come on, short stuff.' She clucked to Bob, who stood and dutifully followed her. It was clear both the dog and her big brother adored her.

'This is my friend, Liz,' Cohen introduced me to his mom and sister when we reached the front porch.

His mom was shockingly young and pretty with high cheek-bones, and big blue eyes. She was a thin bottle-blonde, dressed in a modest coral-colored dress. She gave me a suspicious glance before shaking my hand. Clearly she was nervous about her son bringing a girl home.

'Hi, I'm Liz.'

'Denise,' she offered.

'It's nice to meet you.' I was usually good with parents, but the way she'd already noted my too-long unruly hair, full C's and her son's interest in me. We were off on the wrong foot.

But luckily, after getting Bob settled inside the house, we set off for church.

The service wasn't as bad as I'd expected. I couldn't remember the last time I'd been to church, but I was pleasantly surprised—not that I was ready to make it a regular habit. But there was something comforting about the church itself, and it was nice sitting next to Cohen, especially when he placed his hand on my knee and squeezed after we sat down.

The young pastor delivered a message about the possibility of God being a woman. I'd leaned forward in my seat, along with Cohen's mom and sister, who were clearly intrigued by the idea. Even Cohen's expression was one of genuine interest. I couldn't help but notice and appreciate the fact that having been raised by a single mom, he had strong and healthy relationships with the women in his life.

After the service, Cohen's mom led us to the front of the church. 'There's a really nice girl I want to introduce you to. Pete and Margaret's daughter.'

'Do you mind?' Cohen leaned down to whisper in my ear.

I shook my head quickly, watching as his mother pursed her lips.

'Sure,' he said.

She led the way over to a petite girl standing alone at the front of the church.

'This is Maggie,' Cohen's mother beamed proudly, urging her son forward by placing her hand in between his shoulder blades and giving him a firm push.

'Hey.' Cohen offered her his dazzling smile.

I felt an unexpected pang, like I'd been hit in the stomach.

'Hi.' Her mouth turned up in a small smile, before she trained her eyes to his feet. She had mousy brown hair left unstyled and wore little to no makeup. She looked eighteen, maybe nineteen years old.

'Maggie's a greeter at the mega-mart,' his mom added.

'That's nice,' Cohen said, managing to sound sincere.

I didn't know what was so nice about it, but I kept my mouth shut.

I couldn't help but notice Maggie looked down at the floor. *While the adults were speaking*, I mused.

'This is my good friend, Easy E,' Cohen said, placing his hand on my shoulder.

I elbowed him in the side and we both laughed. His mother frowned. And Maggie looked from Cohen to me, then back to Cohen again, not understanding the inside joke. 'It's nice to meet you…Easy…'

'Call me Liz,' I interrupted offering her my hand. She returned my handshake with a limp-noodle grip.

Though I knew I shouldn't care, somehow it would bug me to see him end up with someone so distinctly lacking in a personality. Plus, she was too young for him. He grew up taking care of his mother and sister; he wasn't your typical twenty-one-year-old college junior. And he needed someone strong and worthy of his love.

'Liz?' Cohen interrupted my thoughts.

'Hm?'

'You ready to go?'

'Oh, yes.'

'It was nice meeting you.' I nodded to the meek girl, and let Cohen's hand on the small of my back guide me toward the exit.

After dropping off his mom and sister, we were back on our way into the city. During the drive, I couldn't help but reflect on the fact that that Cohen's willingness to introduce me to his mother was unexpected. I felt like my own family background was best pushed under the rug and not dealt with. Ashlyn hadn't even met my parents in all the years I'd known her.

'What are you thinking about?' Cohen patted my knee, drawing me out of my serious line of thinking.

'I was just remembering that you owe me breakfast. I'd like pancakes. Now, please.' I smiled, letting some of the tension fall away.

He chuckled. 'You got it. Let's just ditch Boo Boo first.'

If only it was as easy to ditch bad memories. I shrugged that thought off and instead pictured a stack of fluffy flapjacks oozing with butter and syrup. Pancakes weren't a cure-all, but sharing them with Cohen would certainly make my day a whole lot better.

Chapter 7

I was sitting in the center of Cohen's bed, jabbing frantically at the buttons on the game controller, and waving my arms wildly as if that would control the race car on the screen, when my cell chimed signaling the arrival of a new text message.

I dropped the controller and reached for my phone, ignoring Cohen's chuckle as he calmly maneuvered his car around the track, easily beating me in the game.

The message was from Ashlyn, asking if I wanted to go to the mall to get some things for our upcoming weekend at the lake. I cringed. I'd forgotten I'd agreed to go, and as the date got closer, I started to regret saying yes. Being around Ashlyn and Aiden's loving relationship was hard on me for reasons I didn't care to explore.

Inspiration struck and I sent her a text. *Would it be okay if I invited Cohen this weekend?*

Yeah, good idea! Your room has bunk beds too, she replied.

I left out the detail that Cohen and I had been sleeping in the same bed for over a week now. I turned to Cohen, putting on my sweetest, most persuasive smile. 'Would you be interested in coming to the lake with me and my friends this weekend?'

He nodded. 'Sure. Sounds cool.'

And suddenly a shopping trip with Ashlyn sounded perfect. Though Cohen was fun and easy to be around, I needed some space from him—well, mostly from my unrequited attraction to him. And I could get some sexy clothes to bring along. I bit my lip to avoid grinning.

Cohen flipped through the menu screen and chose another course.

'I want a do-over!' I was just starting to get the hang of it.

'We'll do this track. It's easier.'

I shook my head. 'Oh, you don't need to go easy on me, sugar. I've got this.' My confidence level *sooo* did not match my skill level, but I liked seeing him laugh.

'Well I didn't mean easier, I just meant more *beginner-friendly*.'

The flag dropped and the sound of revving engines flooded his bedroom. 'You're going down.' I bounced on my knees excitedly, causing the bed to shake.

I pressed the accelerator button and watched my car zoom ahead. I peeked over at Cohen. His face was a mask of concentration and his teeth bit gently into his soft bottom lip. Damn, that was distracting.

I focused on the video game once again, and watched as my car sped around the track. 'Cohen, look at me! I'm really doing it.'

He chuckled. 'That's my car, babe. Yours is that one.' He pointed to the lower corner of the screen where another car was repeatedly ramming itself into a wall.

Crap! My cheeks flamed pink and I threw the controller down onto the bed. 'This game sucks.'

Cohen smiled as his car crossed the finish line, then he got off the bed to switch off the game console.

I used his absence to roll over to the warm space he'd occupied and curled up with his pillow. 'I think I'm getting addicted to your bed.'

He smiled and lay down beside me. 'I think my bed is getting addicted to having you in it.'

My heart kicked into high gear. Cohen was lying just inches from me, his gaze locked on mine. I waited breathlessly for him to lean in and kiss me.

As though he'd heard my prayer, he bit his lip again and moved closer.

The shrill sound of his pager pierced the silent room and he instantly pulled back. He grabbed for the device and hit a button, silencing it.

'What is it?'

'Car fire.' He frowned. 'On Fifty-first and Macon.'

'Do you have to go?'

He nodded and leaned down, planting a kiss on my forehead. 'Be here when I get home?'

I nodded, afraid my voice would crack if I spoke.

He was up and out the door before what had just happened even fully registered.

I didn't wait around for a man. Ever. But this was different, I tried to convince myself. Cohen was my friend. Yeah right, in what universe?

I grabbed my phone and headed off to pick up Ashlyn for our shopping trip.

I'd just gotten back from my early-morning run when Ashlyn called to say they'd be arriving shortly to pick us up for the weekend away. I'd dashed upstairs to let Cohen know. I found him still in bed where I'd left him an hour ago, cuddling with Bob. As was becoming our usual habit, I'd spent the night with him. The one marked difference was the worry I felt while waiting for him to get home safely from the car-fire call he attended to, and the relief I felt when he finally made it home, sweaty and exhausted hours later. I giggled when I saw them. 'This is what you do when I'm gone?' I teased.

'Bob, what the—?' He shoved the dog away from him as though he was appalled and tugged me down onto the bed. He wrapped his arms and legs around me, pulling me in tight against him. 'That's better.'

'Cohen, gross. I'm all sweaty from my run.' The jogs I took each morning as an attempt at working off the excess sexual tension in my life were quickly negated by Cohen's attention.

He rubbed his nose along my jaw. 'You smell just fine to me.'

My heart pounded against my chest. This sports bra and tiny pair of shorts didn't provide nearly the barrier needed against his bare chest and soft, warm skin. I needed a cold shower. That, and probably even an appointment with my B.O.B.

His scent was so intoxicating, his bare chest so delicious, I almost forgot my rule about not starting into anything that would remotely resemble a relationship. Almost. If only I could get Cohen on board with the notion of a no-strings hookup.

But Cohen wasn't a hit-it-and-ditch-it kind of guy. Not to mention I had a feeling occasional sweaty sex with him would quickly become an addiction hazardous to my stance on singledom.

'Come on.' I shoved against him. 'Ashlyn and Aiden will be here soon. I don't want them to catch us...doing whatever this is we're doing.'

He sat up and pulled me onto his lap, his face turning serious. 'What are we doing?'

I looked down, fumbling with the twisted sheet. He was easy to be around, sweet to me, kind, good-hearted—all of the things, logically, I knew I should want. But something nagged deep inside me. I couldn't go there. Not with Cohen, not with anyone.

'Eliza?' He tilted my chin up with his finger.

I swallowed hard. 'We're friends, right?'

He laughed, low, under his breath. 'If we're friends, then I'm the friggin' Pope.' He ran a fingertip across the swell of my breasts, pushed together by the spandex sports bra. 'If we're friends, then why do I feel so tempted by you?'

My breath caught in my chest. Just the lightest of touches from him, and my entire body was humming and ready. I swatted at him playfully. 'Come on, we've got to get ready. And I need a cold shower.' I cringed. I hadn't meant to say that last part out loud. Oh, well.

Cohen chuckled again before lifting me off him and rising to begin his weekend packing.

When Cohen left to drop off Bob at his mom's for the weekend, I headed downstairs to shower and get ready, knowing my packing would be a little more involved than throwing a few T-shirts and pairs of boxers into a backpack. I'd intended to do it last night, but Cohen and I decided at the last minute to go see a late movie, and I never got to it. A smile twitched on my lips. Who would have known that he'd move in upstairs and change my whole routine?

I was drying my hair when I heard Ashlyn come in. I switched off the blow dryer and met her in my room.

'You're not even packed,' she commented, lifting my empty suitcase from the floor and setting it on the bed.

She helped me sort through the heap of clothes on my bed. After our trip to the mall, I had several pink bags of new bras and panties. I held up a pair of white cotton boy-shorts. 'What do you think, something more virginal?'

Ashlyn chuckled. '*Riiiight.* Like you could pull off virginal.'

I frowned and tossed the panties at her. 'Maybe something a little more daring to get his blood flowing to the right place.' I held up a minuscule black G-string with a glitzy pink heart over the crotch.

'Nothing says stripper like glitter on your underpants.'

I stuffed the panties and a few matching bras into my suitcase. At least then I'd have options.

I added a few tank tops and shorts to the pile of clothes, and went to grab my bathroom bag. When I returned to my room, Aiden had joined Ashlyn in my bedroom.

'Hey, bud.'

'How are you, beautiful?'

I smiled at his attention and Ashlyn grinned at him too. He had that rare ability to make everyone around him feel comfortable and happy. I knew from Ashlyn that his memory had never fully returned, which made him even more set on living each day to its fullest without regrets.

Ashlyn picked up the string of condom packages sitting on my bed. 'What the hell are these? You better not be planning to take that boy's virginity.'

Aiden's eyes went wide, and he held up his hands. 'None of my business. I'll wait in the car.' He picked up my suitcase and left.

I grabbed the condoms from Ashlyn and stuffed them into the drawer on my nightstand. 'Better?' Knowing it was a conversation I wasn't going to win, I let it drop and followed Aiden out of the room.

The three hour drive into Michigan was relatively uneventful. Ashlyn and I sat together in the backseat to chat, and Aiden and Cohen kept up a steady conversation in the front on topics ranging from sports to the stock market to local microbreweries.

Cohen wasn't a typical undergrad, and actually fit in well with our group. He worked full time in addition to being a student, and that seemed to make him more relatable to Aiden. It was nice to see Cohen getting along so well with everyone, and I realized I was feeling proud and satisfied of that fact. To avoid dwelling on that thought I turned to Ashlyn and started talking about research for school.

When we pulled up to the lake house, my jaw hit my lap. This was much more than a little cabin on the shore. It was a large craftsman-style home with a wraparound porch and stunning views of the endless crystal-blue lake.

The guys grabbed the bags while Ashlyn and I jogged up the steps to the porch. The house was gorgeous. Gourmet kitchen, rustic dining table, a huge sectional couch and a large TV. The master bedroom was downstairs with an attached bath, complete with a whirlpool tub. Aiden set their bags on the large bed. Then we toured the upstairs, which was an open loft containing the twin bunk beds for Cohen and I.

Cohen turned to me and smiled 'Top or bottom?'

I entertained myself for a moment with inappropriate images of riding Cohen like a bucking bronco, alternating with images of him hovering over top of me, and gripping his shoulders while he thrust deep inside of me.

'Hm?' I asked, innocently, when I realized Cohen was staring at me, a bemused expression on his face.

'Top or bottom bunk?' he repeated.

Way to burst my fantasy. 'Top.'

Ashlyn bit back a grin. She knew how my mind worked.

We had our own bathroom up there too, with a large double-vanity sink and a glass-enclosed shower. It was nice, yet simple.

After a few more trips out to the car, the kitchen island was loaded with grocery bags and more bottles of wine than we could possibly consume in two days. Ashlyn and I quickly worked to stock the fridge and cabinets with enough food to feed a small village.

Since it was still early afternoon, we decided to head down to the beach. Ashlyn and I made sandwiches while the guys dragged beach chairs out from the shed and situated them on the shoreline. Ashlyn carried the plate of roast beef sandwiches, while I carried a small cooler of beer.

When we reached the guys, they'd each stripped off their T-shirts and sandals.

'Wow, look at that view.' I nudged Ashlyn.

'Yeah, the water's so blue,' she agreed.

'I meant the guys.' I laughed at her innocence. As if noticing to the two shirtless hotties in front of us for the first time, she grinned.

Aiden was a little bulkier and more filled out, and his two tattoos were sexy. Cohen was leaner and hot as fuck. A rush of wetness dampened my bikini bottoms. This was going to be one excruciatingly long weekend. I squeezed my knees together and dropped the cooler unceremoniously in the sand at their feet, Cohen hopping out of the way in time to salvage his toes.

Ashlyn giggled at me and passed out the sandwiches to the guys.

I stripped off my tank top and shorts, grabbed a beer and slid down low into the chair. I hoped my dark sunglasses would keep my perusal of Cohen's body incognito. I struggled with the twist-off top on the bottle of beer until Cohen, who I didn't think had been paying me any attention at all, leaned over and removed the bottle from my hands. He easily twisted the top, his forearms flexing as he did so, then handed it back to me.

'Thanks,' I mumbled. In order to survive this weekend I was going to need alcohol. And a lot of it.

Chapter 8

At sunset Ashlyn and I sat on the deck watching the guys grill steaks. We gossiped and stared at their backsides while they discussed grilling techniques. It felt very domestic being here, coupled up like this. It had been a long time since I'd been part of a couple. But I had to remind myself that Cohen and I weren't a couple. I tucked my legs underneath me and wrapped my arms around my knees, fighting off the chill. A glass of red wine sat untouched in front of Ashlyn, but I was on my third. I was serious about this whole getting-drunk-and-staying-drunk thing this weekend. It was my only defense against Cohen.

At that thought, he looked my direction and frowned. I hadn't spoken to him much today, whether that was on purpose or not, I wasn't sure. But he and Aiden seemed to hit it off well and Ashlyn and I stuck together too, which felt good. She was with Aiden so much lately, it was nice to get some girl time in.

Cohen disappeared inside the house and came back carrying his navy-blue fire department sweatshirt. He held it out to me. 'Cold, babe?' Instead of answering, I took the proffered hoodie and slid my arms inside the sleeves, snuggling into the warmth. I fought the urge to bring it to my nose and inhale. Why was he always doing thoughtful things for me? And more importantly, why did that bug me?

Cohen pulled the hood up, and kissed the tip of my nose. 'Better, Easy E?'

I nodded, obediently.

Ashlyn gave me a strange look, whether it was because of the nickname or Cohen's taking care of me, I wasn't sure. But thankfully, she didn't say anything about it at that moment.

When the steaks were ready, the guys served us at the table. Aiden setting a plate in front of Ashlyn with a kiss and Cohen delivering my plate with a bow. 'Eliza.'

'Eliza?' Ashlyn looked at me quizzically. 'I never knew your name was Eliza.'

I shrugged. 'Cohen. He insists on calling me that.' I couldn't help the smile that crept onto my lips.

After dinner we sat inside on the leather sectional, soft music playing in the background. Ashlyn and Aiden cuddled together in the center, which left Cohen and I sitting on the two furthest ends, apart from each other. I sipped my wine, and scrolled through Ashlyn's iPod, skipping through her playlists to find something I liked. Each time I looked up, I couldn't help but notice Cohen's eyes were on mine. I felt the tingle of butterflies dancing in my stomach, but told myself to let it go. He knew what he was looking for—and it wasn't me.

About an hour later, Ashlyn suggested that we go in the hot tub out on the deck, and we all went to change. Cohen and I headed upstairs to our shared loft bedroom. He grabbed a pair of swim trunks from his backpack and went into the bathroom. I pulled my string bikini out from my suitcase and laid it out on the bed. I took my time undressing, finding I was a little uncoordinated from the wine, and buzzing with the secret desire that Cohen would catch me half-naked.

I removed my tank top and bra, and laid them on top of my suitcase. My breasts felt achy and full, and hungry for Cohen's mouth and hands. Next, I slid off my shorts and panties and stepped into the plum-colored, barely-there bikini bottoms. I didn't hear any sounds coming from the bathroom, but it was still easy to imagine what Cohen would look like undressed. I'd seen him without a shirt plenty of times, and just that was enough to send my libido into overdrive. He was perfect. I draped the bikini top across my chest, just when the bathroom door opened.

'Oh, sorry.' Cohen's voice sounded thick and deep behind me.

'It's okay. Can you tie me up?' I turned to face him, holding the cups in place over my breasts, and watched as Cohen's gaze caressed my bare skin.

'Sure,' he murmured.

I turned so my back was facing him and he gently gathered up the strings and began tying them. The brush of his fingertips against my skin caused me to break out in chill bumps.

'Cold again, babe?' Cohen ran one fingertip down my spine, and I was so desperate for his touch I nearly whimpered. 'Come here,' he whispered, so close I could feel his breath on the back of my neck.

I turned to face him and standing barefoot, I barely cleared his chin. He gathered me up into his arms and pulled me in close. The contact of his bare chest against mine was heavenly. My soft curves molded to his firm body easily. I felt him swallow roughly, and then he separated us, the moment becoming too intimate between us. I sensed Cohen's will weakening, but even more than that, I was starting to have real feeling for him. Which is why when he removed me from his embrace by holding me at arm's length, I didn't protest.

'Come on, they're probably waiting for us.' He tugged my hand, harder than necessary, and led me to the stairs.

After grabbing some towels, we headed out onto the deck and found Aiden and Ashlyn already in the hot tub.

I slipped into the warmth and let out a groan. It felt amazing. It was a beautiful night, starlit and balmy-warm.

Cohen followed me into the hot tub, which instantly felt smaller when he was situated just a foot from me.

Ashlyn scooted onto Aiden's lap and threw her arms around his neck. 'This is fantastic. Thanks for thinking of this getaway for us.'

He gave her a quick kiss. 'Of course, baby.'

I twisted my hair in a bun and sank down further into the water, letting it cover my shoulders, hoping the heat would relax me. Cohen glanced at me and smiled. It was more of a nervous grin than anything else.

After a few minutes of soaking and a whispered conversation, Ashlyn and Aiden climbed out of the water, saying they were going to call it a night, which left Cohen and I sitting alone in the hot water. We sat quietly for a while, just enjoying the stillness of the night. A few minutes later, the silence was broken by voices.

Voices that were making gasping and moaning sounds.

Oh my.

I turned to look at the cabin, realizing the window facing the deck was Ashlyn and Aiden's bedroom. And the window was open. Ashlyn's cries grew in volume until she finally choked out, 'Ah, Aiden, you're so big.'

Cohen's eyes widened and locked on mine. He pulled in a deep breath and shook his head. 'Wow, they're really going at it in there.'

I chuckled nervously. 'Sounds like it.'

Ashlyn and Aiden's loud fucking continued for several minutes, and with each passing second, the vibe around Cohen and I grew heavier, and more intense.

'I need a drink. Do you need a drink?' Cohen said, suddenly standing and exiting the water.

'Um, sure. I'll take a wine.'

I reached over and turned the jets on, which drowned out a fraction of the noise. I considered pressing myself up against the bubbling stream of water to relieve some tension, but instead took a deep breath and clenched my thighs together.

I couldn't help but be reminded of the time I'd walked in on their lovemaking in Ashlyn's living room. I'd made a joke of it at the time, leaning against the wall munching on crackers as I watched, simply because I wouldn't have been able to otherwise process what I saw without downplaying it. It was the most passionate, uninhibited display of love I'd ever witnessed. And it scared the shit out of me. I'd acted cool and like I found the whole thing funny as a way to fool myself into believing that it was put on, an act. But what I witnessed between them was seared into my memory. You found love like that maybe once in a lifetime, if you were lucky.

Cohen returned a second later with our drinks and slipped back into the water with me. 'Damn, it's even louder inside.'

'I'll bet.' I took the glass of wine from him and immediately took a healthy swig. Despite my best attempts at getting and staying buzzed today, the intensity of my attraction to Cohen seemed to keep me mostly sober.

Positioned directly across from him, I couldn't help but notice his eyes lingering on my breasts. I sat up straighter, pushing them above the waterline and Cohen nearly choked on his beer. I bit my lip to avoid smiling. His weakness was so easy to exploit.

The loud groans and noises of energetic sex continued and even ramped up a notch when Aiden and Ashlyn's headboard started banging against the wall.

Unable to escape the erotic sounds, I found myself getting more and more turned on. I couldn't help that a drop of silky heat dampened my bikini bottoms. It was a very intimate experience, hearing every moan, every gasp and grunt, and I knew it was affecting us both. Cohen shifted in his seat, with an uncomfortable look on his face. He alternated his attention between his beer and staring down into the water. But twice more I caught him looking at my chest. Oh God, how badly I wanted him to do something about it. I imagined him tackling me and stripping me of my bathing suit, and bending me over the edge of the hot tub.

When the sounds reached an ear-deafening level for a final outburst from Ashlyn, and then finally died down our eyes met again. It was almost comical how thick with tension the air around us had gotten. But neither of us laughed.

'Think it's safe to go in?' I asked.

He nodded stiffly.

I climbed out of the hot tub first and draped a towel around my shoulders. I turned to hand Cohen a towel as he was coming out of the water, and there was no avoiding it. He was hard as a rock. He grabbed the towel from me and held it in front of himself, where his thick erection strained against the swim shorts.

I thought maybe we'd joke about the awkwardness of the moment—of listening to my best friends fuck at top volume—but his face was serious, his jaw set tense.

He took off past me into the house without another word.

I stood there, stunned at what had just happened. Cohen was turned on. And he desperately wanted to get away from me.

He didn't trust himself around me.

The thought was intoxicating. I headed inside to find him.

I wouldn't push things farther than he wanted them to go. We didn't have to have sex. But that didn't mean we couldn't have a little fun in the meantime. We were attracted to each other, and we were adults. Period.

I crept through the now silent house, feeling strangely alive—all my senses were heightened in my search for Cohen and with the thought of what might happen next. I headed up the stairs to our loft while nerves prickled my skin and an entire colony of butterflies danced inside my stomach.

It was quiet and empty when I reached our bedroom, but I could see light coming from behind the closed bathroom door.

Summoning my courage and feeling bolder than I should, I knocked on the door. 'Cohen?'

'Go away, Liz.' His voice was muffled, but the tone was clear. He wanted to be left alone. And I couldn't help but notice that I was Liz now.

'Cohen, please open the door.'

I waited and practically felt him making the weighty decision, one that would forever change our relationship. A second later the lock clicked and the door opened just a crack. He wasn't exactly inviting me in, but leaving the choice up to me. If that made him feel better, then so be it. I knew what I wanted.

I pushed the door open and found him standing at the vanity in front of the mirror. His erection seemed to have grown, if that was even possible, and I could see his pulse thrumming in his neck.

My heart almost broke. I wanted to touch him, to make this better, to relieve his aching tension. 'Cohen,' I whispered. 'Let me.'

His eyes fell closed at the sound of my voice, and everything my words implied. He turned to face me, and I reached for his waistband and nimbly began undoing the tie that held his shorts together.

He swallowed roughly. I could see him deciding if he should stop me. 'Eliza…'

'Shh. Let me take care of it. Please.'

He groaned in relief.

With the tie now free, I eased the shorts down low on his hips, and his impressive erection jutted out in front of him. My knees buckled with the desire to drop down and take him into my mouth. But I couldn't rush this. I couldn't rush him. I wanted this too badly.

He was beautiful. His thick cock was tense and begging for attention. 'What do you want?' I whispered, looking up at him.

He brought his hand to my jaw and rubbed a slow circle along my skin. 'Touch me.'

I brought my hands to his sides and trailed them down his belly and over the soft trace of hair below his navel. When I gripped his shaft, he sucked in a deep breath and held it. His cock was warm and solid in my palm. I trailed the pad of my thumb over the swollen head, spreading the bead of fluid that had already accumulated there.

I stroked him slowly savoring the newness, the feel of him, watching the way his chest rose and fell. It'd been a long time since I'd given a hand job but I was bound and determined to make this the best damn hand job ever.

His hand hadn't left my jaw, and he pulled me in to his mouth and kissed me, soft at first, then parting my lips to stroke his tongue with mine.

His kiss was intoxicating. The warmth of his mouth, the skilled way his tongue flirted with mine. Knowing we probably weren't going to have sex heightened all my senses and my brain commanded that I pay attention to every touch, each sensation, it was a completely different experience than I was used to. It was all about the buildup rather than a single moment of bliss.

I pushed him toward the vanity so his backside was leaning against the edge of the counter, and tugged his shorts lower. It was time to get down to business. I couldn't wait any longer to have his beautiful cock all to myself and watch him spurt all over his stomach.

I reached behind him into my bathroom bag on the counter. I found the bottle of coconut tanning oil I'd brought and squirted some into my palm. The oil instantly warmed on my skin and when I brought my hand to him, he inhaled sharply. 'Fuck, Eliza,' he breathed, pulling me closer by the back of my neck. I smiled as his lips met mine.

The scent of coconut surrounded us as I worked my hand up and down his cock. 'Oh fuck, fuck, that feels amazing babe,' he whispered. My lips curled into a devilish grin and I kissed him again.

I felt his hands tugging at the strings of my bikini top, and I almost laughed, surprised it had taken him this long to go for them. Once the top was untied, it fell free to the floor and I stood before him, pushing my naked chest out for his appraisal.

I slowed my pace while he drank me in. He swallowed roughly and brought both hands up to cup my breasts, rubbing his thumbs over my nipples. The desire reflected in his eyes shot a throbbing pulse straight to my clit. God, I wanted this man. I wanted him to make me his.

He dipped his head to kiss my breasts, pressing them together with his palms. He ran his tongue along my cleavage, teasing me. I wanted to feel his mouth on my hardened nubs, but he continued his soft, tortuous kisses. I wanted more, so much more, but if this was all I could have, I would take it, eagerly.

He continued nibbling and sucking on my breasts while my oil-slicked palm slid up and down between us.

My breasts jiggled with the effort of pumping my hand up and down, and our movements reflected back at us from the mirror made the experience all the more intimate. There was no hiding, no closed eyes, and no darkness to shield us.

Without warning he groaned out his release, burying his face in my neck.

I watched as a puddle of warm, white semen squirted onto his stomach and mine. We were both breathing hard when he kissed me.

'Why'd you do that?' he whispered against my lips.

'Because I wanted to.'

He grabbed a handful of tissues and cleaned me off first, then himself.

'What about you?' he whispered.

My heart rate skyrocketed, but I tried to appear composed as possible, shrugging at his question rather than answering it directly. I was desperate for his touch, but only if he wanted to touch me.

He kissed my lips softly then bent down, pressing damp kisses along my collarbone. He lowered himself farther to thoroughly suckle at each of my breasts, before dropping to his knees in front of me. I tossed my head back, in complete amazement at his talented mouth. He worked his way lower, kissing my belly, my hip bones. My heart was beating so erratically it felt like it was about to burst from my chest.

He gazed up at me and began untying the strings at my hips. My bikini bottoms fell away, and I found myself extremely thankful that I'd made time for my monthly waxing appointment the previous week.

He leaned forward and kissed my bare mound, teasing and moving lower with each kiss. My eyes were glued to him. He was beautiful and perfect, his dark eyelashes resting against his cheeks, and his full mouth against my most delicate parts.

'Cohen,' I moaned in frustration, shifting my hips closer. I prayed he knew what he was doing, because I felt like I was about to combust.

He opened his eyes and grinned up at me with a sexy half-smile. Then he gripped my hips and hauled me in close to his face. My knees nearly gave out when I felt his warm tongue lapping at my folds.

Holy shit!

I gripped his hair in my fingers and pressed him even closer, pushing my hips forward, greedy for more. He let out a breathy moan at my very direct instructions, but his tongue didn't let up and he suckled, nipped and licked me up and down, spreading my folds apart with his thumbs and driving me completely insane. I didn't know how he was doing what he was doing to me, but holy mother of God, it felt amazing. This boy might not have had sex before, but he clearly had practiced some other things.

Within a few minutes I was on the verge of coming, but felt like my knees were about to buckle any second. I struggled to stay upright, gripping the counter in front of me as the pressure built.

Cohen stopped suddenly and looked up at me. 'Breathe, babe.'

I sucked in a breath, my chest rising rapidly. I hadn't realized I'd been holding my breath, and found it curious that Cohen had noticed even while his attention was otherwise diverted.

He smirked, and then brought his mouth to me again, the broad plain of his tongue darting out to taste me. My groans grew louder, and I tugged at Cohen's hair, crying out his name with each precious flick of his tongue.

Just as my orgasm came my legs finally gave away, but Cohen was ready for it, holding me securely by my waist as he continued his slow torture, drawing out the last of my pleasure.

Chapter 9

My body hummed with euphoria after that orgasm of epic proportions and I was so dazed that I couldn't even feel embarrassed about being completely naked. We made our way clumsily into the bedroom and Cohen helped me into one of his T-shirts. He held firmly onto my hips, helping me, while I climbed up the ladder to the top bunk. As I felt a cool breeze tickle my backside, I was suddenly reminded I wasn't wearing any underpants—and I didn't even want to know what kind of view Cohen had.

Once I was lying down, Cohen leaned over the side of the bunk and kissed my forehead. 'Goodnight Eliza.' He tucked the covers around me securely before retreating to the bed below.

I settled in, drunk on Cohen's touch and the aftereffects of my crippling orgasm combined with the many glasses of wine I'd consumed. I couldn't help but notice the light scent of coconut oil was still on my skin and I smiled a sleepy grin. I knew I'd never look at that bottle of tanning oil the same way again. I would always envision Cohen's parted lips and that string of soft curse words when I coated him in the warm oil. I curled onto my side, still smiling, and drifted off almost instantly.

When I woke the following morning, bright light streamed in through the loft windows and I flung the covers off me, sure I had overslept.

I noted Cohen's bed was rumpled, but empty, and I headed into the bathroom. My discarded bikini lay in the center of the floor and I grinned when I remembered Cohen stripping it off me last night.

I inspected myself in the mirror as I brushed my teeth. My hair was a hot mess. The steam from the hot tub last night had curled the strands around my face, and it looked like an entire family of rodents had taken up permanent residency somewhere around the back and sides. I shrugged, and flipped off the bathroom light. It was hopeless.

I pulled on a pair of panties and shorts, but left on Cohen's soft T-shirt, and made my way down the stairs.

It was silent downstairs and I wondered where everyone was. Thankfully there was a pot of coffee already brewed and I poured myself a cup before investigating.

I took a sip of the hot, blissfully strong coffee, and headed out onto the deck. I found the three of them lounging in the cushy club chairs on the deck, mugs in hand.

When I got closer, they erupted in laughter, and Ashlyn was wiping tears from beneath her eyes. I felt like I was intruding, and not privy to their inside joke.

I felt Ashlyn's eyes appraising me with curiosity and I looked down, surveying myself. I was still in Cohen's shirt, which was so long it concealed the fact that I was indeed wearing shorts underneath it. I unconsciously tugged at the hem, urging it lower. I could tell Ashlyn was wondering what had happened between Cohen and I that left me exhausted, and dressed in his shirt. I didn't feel the need to explain myself to her, especially after her and Aiden's insanely loud fucking.

'Come here, Easy E.' Cohen patted the seat next to him and I slid into it, curling my knees up under me and quietly sipping my coffee.

'How long have you guys been up?' I asked to no one in particular. I couldn't help but noticed they were all dressed.

'A couple hours,' Ashlyn said, absently trailing her hand along Aiden's forearm.

Aiden planted a kiss on her palm and then stood. 'Come on, Cohen. Let's make these beautiful ladies some breakfast.' I grinned up at him. I could see how it'd been easy for Ashlyn to fall for him, amnesia or not.

Cohen gave me a smile, and then headed in behind Aiden.

The grin faded from my face the second I met Ashlyn's eyes. 'What the hell was that, Liz?'

'What was what?'

She cocked her head and continued to glare at me. 'You wake up late dressed in Cohen's clothes, and he's in a *damn* good mood this morning. What happened between you two last night?'

I ran my fingers through my hair, trying to tame the craziness. 'We didn't have sex if that's what you mean.'

'But something happened?'

'Yeah, something happened. After listening to your damn moans and bedpost knocking against the wall for thirty minutes straight, we were a little hot and bothered. Cohen got out of the hot tub sporting a giant erection and I followed him inside and... took care of it.'

Her jaw dropped.

I hadn't meant to make it sound like I was performing an act of public service—trust me, I'd enjoyed *taking care of it*, of him, way more than I should have. I wanted nothing more than to repeat that every day. And the thought of being his first, having him deep inside me, watching the joy and pleasure on his face was enough to get my mind to dive straight back into the gutter.

I held up my hand. 'Don't start, okay? We didn't have sex. And I don't think either of us regrets what happened last night.'

'Fine. But this can't happen again, Liz. You're temping him. And I know you don't have much self-control.'

I set down my coffee mug roughly on the side table. 'Enough. Did I counsel you on your relationship with Aiden?'

'Yes.'

I pressed my mouth closed. She was right. But that was different. Aiden was in a mental hospital—under arrest—and I'd been concerned that he was dangerous. It seemed her concern wasn't for me, but for the innocent Cohen. 'I'm going for a walk,' I blurted.

I set off down the deck stairs and stalked off toward the beach. I began walking with no particular destination in mind, just needing some space from Ashlyn and my growing feelings for Cohen. As much as I hated it, Ashlyn was right. I needed to walk away from Cohen before either of us got hurt. But somehow I knew I wouldn't.

I winced as my pace demonstrated the need for a bra. But I hadn't really planned on needing to get away this morning. I crossed my arms over my chest and continued my trek down the beach.

I was so lost in my thoughts that when I finally focused on my surroundings I didn't recognize anything around me. I hadn't kept track of time, and had no idea how far I'd gone. Feeling weary, I plopped down into the sand and lay back, looking up at the blue sky.

I hated that Ashlyn was probably right. I didn't know what I was doing with Cohen. He was a good boy, I was a hot mess. I knew it was a very bad idea to use him or lead him on, because ultimately I wasn't looking for the whole marriage and babies thing, and I was pretty sure he saw that in his future. I thought I was that kind of girl at one time, but not now, not after the accident and everything that followed. Sometimes I wished things had turned out differently, but I knew that was just a wasted effort. I wouldn't dwell on the past. Doing so would never change how things had turned out for me. It was best to accept it and move on.

I took a deep breath and sat up. I spotted Cohen in the distance, jogging down the beach toward me. When he drew close, he lowered himself onto the sand next to me.

'Water?' He held a bottle out to me.

'Thanks.' I accepted it and took a swig, washing the bitter taste of coffee from my mouth.

'Why'd you take off? Is everything…okay?'

I buried my feet into the damp sand, unsure of what to say.

'Are you mad about last night?'

Mad? At him? God, no. I turned to face him, and his blue eyes locked on mine with such honesty I was taken aback. 'Of course not, Cohen. I wanted that. I wanted you.' I still did. 'Is that okay… what happened between us?'

He laughed, a deep, throaty chuckle. 'Hell, yeah. That was much more than okay.'

I smiled up at him like a giddy idiot.

He shook his head. 'Why'd you take off this morning?'

I rolled over and tackled him to the sand, straddling him with my thighs. 'It had nothing to do with you. I'd take a repeat of last night right here if you'd let me.'

He laced his fingers behind his head, relaxing. 'Go for it, babe. I just wish we had that damn coconut oil.'

I chuckled. 'You liked that, didn't you?'

'Fuck, yeah. I think you've spoiled me from jerking off without it from now on.'

Oh God, the image of him alone in his apartment—doing that—I would never be able to sleep alone again, lying in bed imagining him stroking himself.

I snuggled into his neck, the smile still on my lips. 'How did you learn how to…' I paused and swallowed, deciding the best way to word my question. 'You were really good at going down on me. *Way* better than most guys.'

'Really?' He met my eyes, smiling.

Jeez, guys could be so cocky. 'Yeah.'

'I've probably just had enough practice. I haven't had sex, but I've definitely done all the other stuff, Eliza. I am a guy.'

Sometimes I forgot he was regular guy. I wasn't sure when it began, but I realized now I'd placed him on sort of a pedestal.

He sat up suddenly, hauling me with him. I figured it was my cue to crawl off his lap, but his big, warm arms wound their way around my waist. He pulled me in closer and breathed in against my neck. 'What am I doing with you, Eliza?' he whispered against my skin.

I didn't know if it was a rhetorical question, or if he was expecting an answer, but I remained still and just let me hold me while I could.

'Easy E?' He pulled back and looked at me with confusion. 'What is this? What do you want?' His voice was deep and heavy.

I swallowed roughly, and laid my palm on his roughened cheek. 'Cohen. I'm not the churchgoing, white-picket-fence type that you're looking for.'

His eyes never wavered from mine. 'Then maybe I'm looking for the wrong thing.'

My stomach dropped.

'Cohen…' Any further protests were cut short, because his mouth made its way to mine and he kissed me passionately, holding the back of my neck, weaving his fingers underneath my hair.

If Cohen wasn't going to fight this thing between us, then I wasn't either. I gripped his shoulders and crushed his mouth to mine.

Several minutes later Cohen stood, still holding me against him. He kissed me once more, and set me on my feet. 'Come on, we better get back.'

I couldn't help but grin at him, noting that he had an erection again. I chuckled and laced my fingers with his as we started back to the lake house.

*

Cohen and Aiden were seated at the dining room table playing a heated game of cards, while Ashlyn and I cooked dinner. Well, I cooked salmon and prepared greens for a salad, while Ashlyn fidgeted nervously near the counter. I removed a chef's knife from her hands, sure she was about to slice one of us open.

'Why don't you get the guys another beer and a snack? Dinner will be a bit yet.' It didn't take long at all to prepare salmon and salad, but babysitting Ashlyn was adding time to the meal and I just wanted her out of the room for a minute. She was a major liability in the kitchen. Luckily for her though, Aiden loved to cook.

'I'm on it.' She nodded. She grabbed two bottles of the specialty micro-brewed beer that we'd learned the guys shared in common as their favorite and then began pouring a mixture of different salty snacks into a bowl, balancing it all in her arms to carry it to the table.

I grated lemon rind into a small bowl and added a drizzle of olive oil, adding this flavoring to the salted and peppered pink flesh of the fish.

I glanced up and watched as she delivered the beers and snacks to the table. She exchanged the full beers for the empty bottles and Cohen eagerly dug into the snacks, grabbing a handful and tossing it into his open mouth.

I smiled and hummed to myself, appreciating the cozy domestic vibe this weekend had taken on. I gathered up the empty bags Ashlyn had left on the counter, pretzels, cheese crackers, and salted nuts. *Nuts.*

I rushed toward Cohen and slapped the handful of snacks from his hand. They scattered all over the floor.

'What the—?' Aiden stood to avoid the scattered mess falling into his lap.

I thumped against the back of Cohen's head, and held my hand in front of his mouth, coaxing him to spit the half-chewed bite into my palm.

He did so without question, but the collective intake of breath from Aiden and Ashlyn was almost comical.

'Nuts?' Cohen asked once his mouth was clear.

I nodded and disposed of the mess into a napkin.

'Thanks, babe.' He patted my behind.

I released a deep breath I'd been holding, and went back into the kitchen to throw the used napkin away. Ashlyn followed me into the kitchen.

'He's allergic?'

I nodded, washing my hands.

'I'm so sorry—I didn't know.'

'It's okay. He's fine.'

Then why couldn't I stop my hands from shaking? I thrust them under cold water, and leaned against the sink. I didn't even notice him at first, but Cohen had come up behind me and leaned in close, brushing my hair from my neck.

'Thank you,' he breathed against my skin.

A chill ran down my spine at the soft whisper of his voice. I shut off the water and grabbed a hand towel, shoving away from him. 'Just be more careful.'

I turned toward the oven and set the fish inside to broil, needing something to keep me busy and distracted from the rush of emotions I was feeling.

After dinner the guys cleaned up the kitchen while Ashlyn opened another bottle of wine. I wouldn't have thought it'd be possible to drink all the bottles we'd brought, but we were already opening our last one at eight o'clock on Saturday night.

I curled up on the couch, using Cohen's Chicago Fire Department sweatshirt like a blanket. I accepted a glass of white wine from Ashlyn and leaned back, settling in to the couch. This weekend wasn't at all what I had been expecting. I had developed deeper feelings for Cohen, if that was even possible, which left me feeling confused and irritable. And on top of that, each time Cohen did something sweet or thoughtful for me, or each time my eyes lingered on his for too long, I'd catch Ashlyn narrowing her eyes at me.

When the dishes were done, Aiden joined Ashlyn on the couch, and I forced myself to remain facing forward, rather than turn and search for Cohen like I desperately wanted to. A second later, I felt his warm breath at my ear.

'Come upstairs with me.'

My pulse jumped. His silent invitation and everything it implied set my skin on fire. I leaned forward and set my glass of wine down on the coffee table while Cohen disappeared upstairs.

Ashlyn and Aiden were cuddling on the sectional sofa across from me, and I made a show of stretching my arms above my head and yawning. 'I'm beat.'

'It's early still,' Ashlyn said. 'Where's Cohen?' She peeked around the corner into the empty kitchen.

Rather than answering, I stood, leaving the sweatshirt on the couch. 'Well, I think I'm going to call it a night.'

'You can't do this,' Ashlyn hissed under her breath.

Aiden's hand on her forearm relaxed her just slightly. 'Leave them alone. They're both adults.'

I smiled at Aiden and headed for the stairs. My pulse quickened with each riser and when I finally reached the top, I found Cohen lying on the bottom bunk, his hands folded behind his head and a huge smile on his face.

'What are you doing?'

'Shh. Come here.' He moved over in the tiny bed, making room for me.

I slid in next to him, very aware that the loft was open all the way to the lower floor where Aiden and the very disapproving Ashlyn were currently sitting. I snuggled close to his body and his arm snaked its way around me, holding me securely against his side.

He held my hand in his and gently caressed my palm, running his thumb along the creases there. I remembered back to our conversation about my love line, and when he first found out I was damaged goods. Not that I had told him anything useful. Nor would I. He brought my palm to his mouth and placed a kiss directly in the center.

'So…what should we do?'

I faked a yawn. 'I'm pretty tired. Guess I'll just get some sleep.' I closed my eyes, fighting off a smile.

Cohen tickled my sides wickedly, causing me to bite back a squeal and buck off the bed.

'Cohen!' I struggled to maintain my composure and swatted at his chest. The last thing I needed was Ashlyn hearing noises like that coming from up here. I was convinced she wouldn't be above sprinting up here and physically separating me form Cohen. And somehow, that was the most depressing thought ever—one I didn't want to reflect on any longer than was necessary. He caught my hand in his and pressed it firmly against his muscled chest. He chuckled softly. 'Relax, babe.'

I pressed my hand over his mouth. 'Shush.' But his smile was contagious, and soon I was grinning back at him like an idiot. Our eyes met and held for several moments, his filled with something that pulled at my chest. I pushed the feeling aside. I only wanted the physical with him—not the emotional. I couldn't handle going there again. With anyone. Especially someone as perfect and love-able as Cohen. It would only end in heartbreak for us both.

I leaned in closer to him and let my hand fall away from his mouth. 'Are you going to be good?' I whispered seductively against his lips.

He nodded, eagerly. 'Anything for you.'

Oh, and I knew he would be good. He was sexy as hell without even trying. All his lean muscle and manly goodness were almost more than I could handle. Almost.

I pressed my lips to his and kissed him softly. He worked his hand under my hair, holding me firmly to him and parting my lips with his tongue.

I could already tell tonight would be different from last night. It was more of a slow build—every touch meant to soothe, every caress meant to tease, and every kiss meant to excite just a little more than the one before, but there was no catalyst like last night. In some ways I liked it more, because I knew it meant we would explore each other's bodies for longer, without the need for a quick release, but in another way, I didn't like that it felt like something more—something tender to be savored.

Needing to take control and change the emotion of the situation, I pushed Cohen's shoulders down to the bed and climbed on top of him, straddling his lap.

He ran his hands up my sides, lifting my shirt as he went. I raised my arms, encouraging him to remove it completely like I knew he wanted to.

His fingers skimmed lightly over the pale-pink bra I wore, dipping in between the curves, and tracing the hardened nubs beneath the fabric. My breaths came in shallow, more ragged, bursts. He watched my eyes the entire time, seeming to like the reaction he got from me, but I could tell this slow build was affecting him too. His jeans were tight across his hips and straining between us.

He finally reached back to release the clasp. My bra fell free and his sharp inhale caused a swell of pride to surge through me. Cohen's callused hands covered my breasts with less finesse than before, as if he couldn't restrain himself any longer, but his touch was no less exquisite. I let out a barely contained moan, not because of the sensation itself, but because of how thoroughly Cohen was enjoying himself. He leaned up on one elbow, and pressed his other hand into the small of my back, urging me to lower my breasts to his mouth. When his warm, wet tongue met my nipple and he sucked, hard, the groan that escaped my lips was most definitely of pleasure.

'Cohen,' I breathed.

His mouth pulled from my nipple with a suckling sound and he met my eyes. 'Shh,' he reminded me.

I bit my lips, my cheeks reddening. I had forgotten about our surroundings—the open loft and the bedroom that was within earshot of our friends downstairs.

'Do you like it, babe?'

'Yes. Please keep going.'

He grinned and brought his mouth to my other breast, licking and teasing me while still meeting my eyes. But when I pressed my hips against his, his eyes fell closed and he released a strangled groan before pulling my nipple into his mouth.

I continued to writhe against him, teasing his hard cock between us and wishing we were naked.

After he had thoroughly feasted on my breasts and they were damp with his kisses and pinkened from the stubble of his jaw, I lowered myself, wiggling down his body until I was face-to-face with his belt buckle.

He swallowed roughly and lifted up on his elbows to watch me.

I took my time, tracing the outline of his erection with a single fingertip, before slowly unbuckling his belt, and tugging down his zipper inch by inch in anticipation of the mouthwateringly delicious cock waiting for me.

Even though I was sure that what I was doing could probably be described as a form of torture, Cohen didn't complain. He didn't help free his cock from his boxers, or push me to move me along faster. He just continued to watch me as though he was captivated, both lust and wonder reflected in his beautiful blue eyes.

I nibbled at the outline of his erection through the boxer briefs, using my teeth to lightly nip and tease him. His breathing quickened and his chest rose and fell more rapidly.

I finally tugged his boxers down with both hands, and he lifted his hips to allow me to pull both them and his jeans off his legs. He yanked his T-shirt over his head and tossed it to the floor.

He was completely naked, and his body was holy-God-wow. I sucked in a deep breath, noticing that my panties were already soaking wet, and probably even my shorts too.

His fingers skimmed across my belly and danced along to the waistband of my little jean shorts, toying and teasing me with his leisurely pace. I'd never hated a button so much in my damn life. He finally freed the button and I lifted my hips so he could pull the shorts down my legs. Then he dropped them to the floor with the rest of his clothes.

I was now only wearing a tiny scrap of fabric—the black g-string I'd packed. It was meant to tempt him, but it was also succeeding in making me feel like a sexy seductress. I didn't trust myself around Cohen. I bent at the waist, lifting my bottom into the air and lowering my mouth to his beautiful cock. He held himself in place with one hand gripped around his shaft while I lovingly stroked my tongue from base to tip, spending more time at the head, noticing that when I flicked my tongue he cursed under his breath, and fisted his other hand into the blanket.

I kissed the back of his hand and removed it from his shaft, then I wrapped both hands firmly around him and began pumping up and down, suckling the head at the same time. He groaned and closed his eyes. 'Fuck, babe. Fuck, fuck,' he whispered.

I smiled at the naughty endearments.

I felt Cohen grab my ass and squeeze, gripping one fleshy cheek as I bobbed up and down with my mouth around his cock. His fingers worked their way under the string on my panties and he began tugging them down.

I stopped suddenly and sat up. 'Cohen, those have to stay on, or nothing is going to stop me from riding your cock.'

He groaned and his head fell back against the pillow. 'Fuck,' his chest rumbled with the curse. 'Don't say stuff like that, babe.'

'Cohen.' My voice was a plea, only I didn't know what for. He was supposed to be the strong one. I wasn't known for my will-power, but for him, I would try.

He left my panties in place, but pulled me onto his lap again. I wanted the contact against him just as much as he did. He rocked his hips against mine, and pressed his cock against my soaked panties with each thrust. I leaned over him, and let my breasts sway gently against his chest while we kissed. The feel of my nipples skimming over his pecs was another of the sensations that I normally wouldn't have noticed. His kisses were rough and desperate, his tongue matching the pace of his thrusts. It was hypnotic and sensual. Another thing to love about Cohen.

I'd never come just from dry humping before, but damn if I wasn't close to orgasm already. I could tell from his breathing that he was too.

Just one tiny little piece of dampened fabric separated us, and I imagined what it would be like to have his impressive cock sink inside me. I would only need to push the panties aside and he could fill my empty pussy. 'Cohen, I want you inside me,' I blurted without thinking.

His entire body went stiff and I could read the conflicting emotions on his face as clear as day. He pressed his lips to mine one last time, and then sat up and moved me off him.

Shit. Had I said the wrong thing?

He flipped us over, so that I was lying flat against the bed, and he was hovering over me. He spread my thighs, forcing them apart and kneeled on the bed between my legs.

He pulled my panties aside, but left them on. The strings cut into my hips, but I didn't even really notice. He rubbed his thumb along my clit, gently stroking and teasing. Oh Lord, I was so close. He brought one finger to my entrance and slowly pressed forward. I sucked in a breath and held it as he gently eased his finger out and in, out and in, adding a second finger to the first. I groaned at the pressure, and his version of being inside of me. This wasn't what I had in mind, but I realized it would have to do. And damn if it didn't feel amazing.

I reached between us and stroked him while he continued to pump his fingers in and out of me. I watched his movements as he continued thrusting, the veins in his forearm standing out, his muscles tense. God, was he sexy.

Only a few thrusts later and I was there. I released a breathy moan and called out his name. Cohen clamped one hand down over my mouth to silence my cries as I came. The feel of his hand pressed firmly over my mouth while his other hand continued to drive forward inside me was enough to make me come unglued. I'd never had so much fun *not* having sex.

He let out a soft curse word, and a few seconds later he came, hot and sticky all over my stomach and panties. It was insanely sexy to feel him mark me as his, to feel his juices and mine mingle between my legs.

He collapsed down on top of me and I nestled into his neck and breathed in his masculine scent, knowing that spending much more time around Cohen without fucking him was soon going to be impossible.

Chapter 10

Ashlyn didn't speak to me much in the morning as we packed up the lake house. And by the time we were in the car, with my head resting against Cohen's shoulder, I no longer cared. She wrongly assumed that we were having sex, that I was a heartless hussy stealing poor Cohen's virginity, and I just couldn't find the energy to try to convince her otherwise. Her distrust in me bothered me. Was I not good enough for Cohen?

I closed my eyes and was drifting in and out of sleep to the sounds of the highway humming beneath us and the gentle vibration of the car when we came to a screeching halt.

I sat up quickly, looking around, unable at first to process the chaos around us. Ahead on the highway a car had flipped over on its roof, steam seeping from the engine. Not far away a truck was down in the ditch, lying on its side. A man and a woman were climbing from the cab of the truck, looking battered and shocked.

Before I even realized what was happening, Cohen was no longer beside me. He had dashed from the car and was running toward the scene of the accident, shouting something at Aiden who trailed behind him, already talking on his cell phone.

My heartbeat pounded in my ears and I couldn't tell if I was imagining the sounds of the screams and sirens I heard echoing in the distance.

Ashlyn climbed from the front seat back toward me and we huddled together. I was suddenly freezing and shaking, and I realized she was crying, but I didn't know why. We were okay. Aiden was okay. What was wrong?

That was when I saw it.

Cohen was dragging the body of a woman from inside the overturned car. He lay her down on the road, and shouted something to Aiden, who was standing beside him. Aiden nodded and darted back towards us. He opened the driver's door and reached in with shaking hands to pop open the trunk. 'Aiden, is she okay?' Ashlyn demanded.

'Stay here,' he warned, then disappeared from sight around the back of the car. He returned to Cohen's side a few seconds later carrying a beach blanket.

Cohen draped it across the woman, covering her from head to toe, then crawled back to the car where he appeared to be talking to someone. Was there someone still alive in that car? It didn't seem possible.

My eyes focused for a moment on the contrast of Ashlyn's brightly colored tangerine and pink beach blanket being used to cover the body of a woman I was pretty sure was dead. I had just lounged on that blanket yesterday, basking in the sun without a care in the world, and was instantly reminded of the harsh lesson life had taught me once before. Everything you held dear could be taken from you in the blink of an eye.

Cohen lay on his belly and reached into the smashed up car, and pulled out a little girl who looked to be probably three or four years old. She was crying and blood oozed from a gash to her forehead, darkening the blonde hair at her scalp. Cohen carried her away from the vehicle, cradling her in his arms as she cried and screamed for her mother.

He brought her to the side of the road and set her down on the grass and bent to speak to her before returning to the car once again. A couple of concerned bystanders appeared with blankets, doing their best to calm the hysterical child.

Suddenly I needed air. I needed out of this cramped backseat and I lunged for the door. Ashlyn tried feebly to stop me, but when she saw the look on my face, she released me and fell from the open door onto the gravel, my feet not even able to support my weight. I crawled away from the car on my hands and knees and vomited into the grass. After spitting a few times to clear my mouth, I sat down on the ground, unable to move, unable to think and shaking violently.

The sirens grew louder and several police cars and an ambulance skidded to a stop on the highway. I watched as a stream of uniformed officers and paramedics jogged toward the scene. Cohen met them, and began shouting things and pointing. His face was a hardened mask of concentration, until he scanned the scene and met my eyes. I was sure I looked completely pathetic, sitting in the grass, crying and shaking, but I couldn't even pretend to be strong right now.

He returned to my side and helped me stand, holding my weight up by securing his arm around my waist. He walked me over to Aiden and said something I couldn't hear. Aiden picked me up and carried me back to the car, laying me down on the front seat and covering me with a blanket. I closed my eyes and curled onto my side and bawled. The pain of losing Paul rushed up inside me and overwhelmed everything else. I was transported back five years, the memory of the crushing heartbreak as painful now as it had been then.

Listening to the sounds of horror and grief taking place outside of the car, I knew I could never let myself love Cohen. My throat tightened and I struggled for air. I curled into a ball and wrapped my arms around myself. There was no way I would survive another crushing tragedy, and I renewed the promise I made to myself the night of Paul's death. I had to guard my heart. It was the only way.

Chapter 11

When we finally got home, I was exhausted and emotionally drained. Our journey back from the lake felt more like we'd gone to hell and back. The accident had added a few hours onto our trip, both with Cohen helping to respond at the scene, as well as the resulting traffic backup. The mood in the car had been subdued and quiet, with no one wanting to talk. That had been fine with me.

Aiden and Ashlyn dropped us off, and Cohen insisted on carrying my bags inside. I tried to lift my suitcase from the trunk and found I had lost all muscle strength. Cohen's hands darted in past mine and he easily lifted the bag, hauling it inside for me. I collapsed onto the couch while he heated a mug of water in the microwave and made me a cup of tea, mumbling something about it calming my stomach.

The blissful weekend had taken a violent turn in the blink of an eye. It now seemed a lifetime ago that I'd relaxed in Cohen's arms, that we'd shared some intimate moments. Almost as though they'd never even happened.

Cohen set the mug on the coffee table in front of me, and sat down beside me on the sofa. He rubbed his hands against his knees, lost in thought.

'Cohen, you can go. I'll be fine.'

His eyes met mine and were full of skepticism. 'What can I do to help? Can I run you a bath?'

A bath sounded heavenly, but something in me rebelled, reminding me not to get too close. 'I can manage on my own. I think you should go.'

Getting this comfortable with him so quickly had been a mistake. I was glad we hadn't gone any farther over the weekend. I didn't want him getting confused about my feelings for him. I had tried to convince myself otherwise, but I knew deep down that sex with him would never be emotionless and uncomplicated. I couldn't explain how I knew. I just did. And I couldn't let myself go there with him.

Cohen hadn't yet moved from the couch and was staring intently at the steam rising from the coffee mug.

I stood and dragged my suitcase over to the laundry room off the kitchen, as if to prove to him that I was capable, and I started the washing machine. I was stuffing clothes into the washer without regard for color or fabric when Cohen came up behind me and gripped my upper arms, spinning me to face him. 'What is this? Why do I feel like you're breaking up with me when we're not even dating?'

'Cohen... Please. I just can't. Not with you. Not with anyone,' I mumbled, staring down at my feet.

He tilted my chin up to look at me, and I closed my eyes. I knew it was childish, but if I met his blue eyes, I might crumble. And I couldn't allow that to happen. His hand remained on my cheek, cradling my face and rubbing a slow circle with his thumb near my ear.

When he spoke again, his voice was just a whisper. 'What happened to you, Eliza?'

I waited several seconds before responding. Then I took a deep breath and practiced saying the words in my head before repeating them out loud. 'I lost someone I loved in a car accident.' I didn't tell him the rest. I didn't explain that we were engaged, that I was pregnant when he passed away, that it was my fault that he was driving three hours to see me in Des Moines that night when he fell asleep behind the wheel. I didn't tell him that Paul had also called me Eliza.

'I'm sorry. How long ago?' Cohen asked, his voice still soft, still gentle.

'Five years.'

His hand dropped from my face, and he leaned in to press a kiss to my forehead. 'I'm sorry you had to see that today. I should have stayed with you, I didn't know.'

My eyes flicked to his. 'No, you were right to help. It was just… hard. Being at that scene brought up feelings I never want to experience again.'

He nodded, and pulled me in for a hug. I let my body mold to his, my arms hanging limply at my sides.

Cohen finished adding my clothes to the washer, added some soap and then steered me back to the couch. 'Get some rest, babe. I'll call later to check on you.'

When he walked away, my brain knew putting some distance between us was the right thing to do, but my body instantly ached for his warmth. I curled onto my side, dragging the throw blanket over me and fell into a restless sleep.

When Cohen called later and woke me up, I didn't answer my phone. And when he followed it up with a text to see if I was coming up to stay the night, I responded with an excuse about wanting to stick around for my cats. Not that they even noticed if I was there. As long as food appeared in their bowls, and the sun continued to provide warm spots for them to lounge in, they were content.

Several days passed and I did my best to avoid seeing Cohen. I'd seen him out for an early morning run with Bob a few times, where we'd waved hello, but not spoken. He'd texted me late one night, just a brief line to ask how I was, but it went unanswered and he didn't text again. I don't know if I expected him to put in more effort, but I couldn't help the surprise I felt at how easily and quickly he'd slipped from my life.

And then last Sunday, when I was out for a run, I'd seen him with that mousy church girl Maggie. They were walking back from the diner on the corner. He'd met my eyes and smiled, and when he did, I felt a pang of jealousy stab at my chest.

It was strange how protective I was over his virginity. I wasn't prepared to take it myself, but it made me furious to think of any other woman doing the job instead. I'd stormed inside the house and forced my drapes closed.

Chapter 12

Several more days passed by before I saw Cohen again. The accident and the woman's death continued to weigh heavily on my mind, and I still barely slept at night. But I didn't allow myself to go to Cohen's bed like I wanted to. I knew I needed to stay strong. Seeing the horrific scene at the accident had slapped some much needed sense into me, and reminded me of the need to distance myself from the pain of losing someone. I couldn't go through that again. I wouldn't survive it for a second time.

So instead I focused on getting through each day. Class…studying…feeding my cats…trying to make myself eat something… and then falling into a restless sleep alone in my bed. But my thoughts betrayed me and constantly drifted to Cohen. His soft kisses, his silly nicknames, and even that damn dog Bob.

That was why when Stu called me, I had no reason to say no and was hoping that clocking some action between the sheets would force Cohen from my mind once and for all. But of course, that hadn't been the case. I hadn't been able to go through with it, worrying about if Cohen was home to hear us. At least that's what I told myself, I didn't want to think that my feelings for Cohen were what was really effecting my decision.

Twenty minutes later, I walked out a very unsatisfied Stu, anxious to get rid of him.

Stu clicked the keyless entry for his car, flashing the lights on his Lexus just as Cohen came walking up. I wasn't sure where he'd been, as he was coming from the opposite direction of campus, but I reminded myself that his comings and goings weren't supposed to be my business. His eyes fell on me first, his flirty smile kicking up a notch, but when he noticed Stu—aka Professor Gibson—standing on my porch, his smirk faltered and he looked from us to the house as if he was working out in his mind what had just happened in there.

Shit. My stomach twisted into a knot. Why did I feel so bad? I wanted to blurt out that nothing had happened, that he was jumping to conclusions, but I pressed my lips together. I could have whomever I wanted over at my house, for whatever reason. Right?

I wondered if he'd storm past us to his apartment, but he surprised me by fixing a smile on his face and stopping to say hello. 'Professor.' He nodded to Stu.

Stu straightened his jacket and offered his hand. *God, could he be any more awkward?*

Observing Cohen next to Stu made for a ridiculous comparison. Cohen looked young and relaxed in dark-washed jeans that fit low on his hips, a soft, worn T-shirt that hugged his biceps and a rugged pair of vintage-style navy-blue tennis shoes. He was fucking hot, in a casual and understated way. He wasn't trying, he was just delicious, like the sexy boy-next-door. Whereas Stu, well…he was Stu. He gave off a distinct dad vibe that signaled his divorced status and professional job. He was someone I wasn't even remotely at risk of falling for. Which had been part of the whole attraction in the beginning, but now I knew that that was wrong.

I couldn't help but continue to draw a comparison between fun-loving, playful Cohen and buttoned-up, tassel-loafered Stu. Stu's down-to-business approach to sex hadn't bothered me before, but I realized Cohen made me want something more. That giddy, butterfly feeling that I hadn't allowed myself to feel in so long, I thought I'd forgotten how.

I smiled, knowing I hadn't completely lost it. I thought I'd lost it all when Paul died, but maybe I hadn't. That thought both comforted and terrified me.

But I reminded myself that Stu was safe. Boring, practical and lackluster in bed, but safe. End of story. If it was possible, that thought made me feel worse.

Stu was saying something to Cohen about the midterm, but Cohen looked unconcerned and bored by the whole interaction.

'All right, I guess I'm off. Eliza.' Cohen tipped his head to me.

I dared a look in his direction, just as he passed by me. Anger, sadness, and…something else…was reflected in his eyes. It was that spark, that flame…whatever it was that burned between us.

I swallowed and said goodbye to Stu. That was the other good thing about his visits—no goodbye kiss was needed. I headed back inside, feeling worse than I did before Stu's visit, which had been designed to relieve tension, not cause it.

Chapter 13

I walked home from campus on Friday evening, thankful that the weekend had finally arrived. I had nothing on the agenda but spending some quality time with my couch, bundled up in my comfy pjs with a nice glass of wine. I hoisted my bag up higher on my aching shoulder and mentally reminded myself I was overdue for a massage. And would need another waxing appointment soon. Not that anyone would notice right now. I obviously hadn't seen Cohen and since that awkward night I'd let all of Stu's calls go unanswered.

When I reached the front walk, I couldn't keep myself from glancing up at Cohen's window. His apartment was dark. He was probably out tonight, doing whatever it was undergrads did on a Friday night.

I let myself inside, tossed my bag onto the bench beside my door and collapsed face down on my sofa.

I was somewhere in between sleep and wakefulness when I heard my phone ringing from inside my bag.

I scrambled off the couch and answered on the fourth ring. Not surprisingly, it was Ashlyn.

'I have some crazy big news!' she shrieked. I shifted the phone from my ear, hoping to preserve some of what was left of my hearing.

'So spill it, doll.'

She giggled with excitement. 'Oh, it's too good. I can't just tell you over the phone. Meet me and Aiden for drinks tonight. This is something we need to celebrate.'

'Okay. Where?' To be honest the distraction of getting out for a drink sounded good, and her giddiness was contagious. I could certainly muster up some energy for my best friend, after all.

We made plans to meet up in thirty minutes at a swanky club downtown. It was the same place we went to celebrate last term when Ashlyn's thesis proposal was approved, and the place where she first she introduced Aiden to others, rather than keeping him all to herself in her apartment all the time. Of course, that was back when he was still known as Logan.

I peeled off my clothes and stood undressed inside my walk-in closet. I rifled through the hanging blouses and pencil skirts, but nothing seemed right. I settled on a pair of black skinny jeans and a simple black tank top, along with the tallest pair of heels I owned.

I stood in front of the mirror and twisted my hair up into a sleek bun. I hadn't meant to dress in all black, but I supposed it fit my mood. I added lipstick and blush to wake up my look and grabbed a small leopard-print clutch, then I was on my way.

Several minutes later, I was elbowing my way through a wall-to-wall crowd at Club Aqua cursing Ashlyn's name and regretting my decision to come out.

I should have just made her tell me her big news on the phone. I was pretty sure it had to do with the fact that her thesis was now finalized. She'd reworked it over the last year and had removed all traces of Aiden's case from it. She'd come clean to Professor Clancy about their relationship and explained that she no longer felt right about mixing business and pleasure, so to speak. She didn't ever want her professionalism or judgment called into question, so she spent the last year reworking her whole project. But it'd paid off. I was sure that was what tonight's celebration was about.

She'd already had a few articles published in small journals about amnesia and was really making a name for herself. It was cool to see, but that didn't mean I needed to be out right now, getting groped and having drinks spilled on my beautiful shoes when all I felt like doing was curling up on the couch.

After passing through a crowd of girls surrounding a bridezilla—complete with a veil and tiara—who was shrieking like a banshee, I finally spotted Ashlyn, waving to me from across the room. Her smile was a welcome sight and I made a beeline straight for her.

Over the past few weeks, we'd talked a few times about the car accident we'd witnessed and Ashlyn couldn't erase it from her mind any better than I could, so I was glad to see her looking happy and relaxed tonight. I let the tension fall away as she pulled me into her arms for a hug. I patted her back with one arm. I was never much of a hugger.

When I pulled back, Ashlyn thrust her left hand into my face, a large diamond nearly poking out my eye. 'We're engaged!' she shouted above the music.

I fixated on the ring, in utter shock and disbelief. It was a beautiful round-cut diamond, sparkling and elegant, big enough without being flashy, and set in a band studded with tiny diamonds all around it. I sucked in a breath of air despite the crushing weight I felt on my chest, and knowing I was about to burst into tears, I pulled her in for a hug, holding her longer than necessary in order to pull myself together. Ashlyn pulled back out of my arms, mistaking my tears for happy ones. I was supposed to be happy for her, right? So why did I feel like someone had just punched me in the stomach?

'Oh, sweetie! I know, isn't it great?'

I nodded and wiped at my eyes. 'Congratulations, Ashlyn.' I plastered on a smile. 'Where's the lucky guy?' She grabbed my hand and led me through the crowded bar. I couldn't help but notice the ring felt like a bulky barrier between our hands. That would take some getting used to.

Aiden was standing at the bar, with a glass of amber-colored liquor in his hand, and he was grinning like a damn fool. 'Congrats, bud.' I hugged him as well, lifting up on my toes and snaking an arm around his shoulder.

'Are you sure you're okay with this?' His warm breath brushed past my ear.

He was either more perceptive than I realized, or he was remembering the fact that I didn't approve of him dating Ashlyn in the beginning. 'Yes. She's happy, and that's all I care about. And despite busting your balls early on, I know you're good for her.' I slid up to the bar as they shared another hug. I needed a drink. Preferably something strong.

'Wine? Champagne?' Aiden asked.

I shook my head. 'Double vodka soda,' I shouted to the red-haired girl behind the bar.

I took the drink with shaking hands and tossed the thin black straw aside to knock back a healthy sip.

I tried to enjoy the rest of the night, celebrate with my friends who were happy, in love, and newly engaged, but despite the upbeat atmosphere and the bottomless drinks the bartender seemed to be serving, it all felt hollow somehow. The distinct feeling that someone was watching me compounded my discomfort and caused me to scan the sea of bodies mingling behind me. My heart pounded in my chest as my gaze met his.

Cohen.

He was dressed in jeans and a fitted black T-shirt with the word *Security* printed across the chest in white block lettering. I wanted to run across the room to him, to fling my arms around his neck and inhale his comforting scent, but I stayed put, balanced on the stool, afraid that if I tried to stand, my legs wouldn't support my weight.

The house music thumped in time with my heartbeat, and I began to feel lightheaded. Cohen's eyes traced the length of my body, from my heel-clad feet dangling from the stool, up to my hand circling the glass I was holding. It was as though he could see right through me, to everything underneath, everything I was thinking. Everything I desperately wanted.

I realized I'd been holding my breath, waiting for him to come to me when he pressed the device in his ear, listening to something only he could hear and he set off toward the back of the club. I began breathing again once Cohen disappeared from sight. I glanced at Ashlyn to see if she'd noticed him, but she was happily chatting away with Aiden, obviously oblivious. For a moment I wondered if I'd imagined him, but I was certain I hadn't. I'd felt his hunger for me from across the room, and my body had visibly responded, breaking out in chill bumps despite the heat of the room.

Later, when I'd followed Ashlyn to the dance floor, I'd begun to think I had imagined the whole Cohen-spotting, as there'd been no trace of him again. Aiden stole Ashlyn away from me but I continued to sway to the music, oblivious to everything but the thumping bass and my own heartbeat.

It felt good to let everything fall away, to feel the music and forget everything else. A warm hand on my shoulder snapped my eyes open. For a second I thought it could be Cohen, but the guy looking back at me couldn't have been more different from Cohen if he tried. He was sporting a colorful sleeve of tattoos that covered his entire left arm, and a small barbell was pierced through one eyebrow. Mr. Eyebrow Stud smiled, and rested his hands on my waist, following my movements. I placed my hands on his shoulders and let him guide me. He was pressed close, warm and sexy with his bad-boy looks, and I was drunk. I took a deep breath and let it out slowly, turning myself over to the moment.

His hands skimmed along my hips, holding me close and moving with me. My pulse drummed anxiously in my neck at the thought of Cohen spotting us.

I shimmied against him in time with the music and thought about how effortless it would be to flirt my way into his pants, to get him to come home with me. My brain ran through all of this in a matter of seconds, but I kept my face impassive and aloof. It would be so easy to engage in nameless, faceless, emotionless sex with this guy, but I knew that would only make me feel worse. I knew it wasn't what I really wanted. *He isn't Cohen*, a little voice inside my head pointed out unnecessarily.

When I opened my eyes, Cohen was back, watching me from across the room. Our gazes collided and held. Then his eyes drifted down to Mr. Eyebrow Stud's hands gripping my hips and he frowned, his eyebrows knitting together. Seeing Cohen when all my defenses were down was wreaking havoc on my willpower. I wanted nothing more than to go to him. To touch him, taste him. His icy-blue gaze remained locked on mine, his expression unreadable, and I fought the urge to cross the room.

He pressed a finger to the earpiece again, listening intently and set off for the bar. Even as I danced with another man, my eyes followed Cohen's every moment, the tense way he moved, the stiff set of his shoulders. He reached the bar, and another guy in a black security shirt. He and Cohen exchanged a few words, and then Cohen took hold of a blonde girl near them, steering her by the arm off the stool and across the crowded room, parting the sea of bodies for them as he moved.

He walked down a back hallway, guiding the girl in front of him forward with the hand at the base of her spine until they disappeared from sight. My imagination ran wild, picturing her doing to him what I did just a few weekends ago. The thought made me sick and then cold, hard realization smacked me in the face. This was just what Cohen felt like seeing Stu leaving my house. God, I was a bitch. I had no one to blame for this mess but myself. Well, fate played a hand, too. But she was cold and hard and nasty, and that would never change—no matter how hard I wanted otherwise.

The liquor in my stomach churned violently and suddenly, I had to get away. I stumbled across the dance floor, squeezing past bodies as I went, fighting my way to the restroom.

I was nearly there—alone in a back hallway when a single word pulled me to a halt.

'Eliza.'

Cohen closed the distance between us, and as soon as he was near, all of my resolve disappeared. The drinks had caught up with me, and that, coupled with Cohen's presence and familiar scent, was fucking with my head. 'You work here?' I asked, leaning closer to him, tracing the lettering stretched across his T-shirt with a fingertip.

The girl he was escorting was nowhere in sight, and I realized with a twinge of shame that he was just doing his job, probably depositing an over-beveraged patron into the restroom.

His hands darted out to steady me, gripping my hips as I wobbled in the impossibly high heels, and I clutched his biceps for support. 'I thought I told you I worked security at a club.' His words were hollow, and efficient, like he wanted to get this conversation over as soon as possible.

I nodded, remembering that he had. I just hadn't known it was this club. This place was known to be a meat market. I was sure drunk girls were constantly throwing themselves at him. I pushed the errant thought away. He wasn't mine, and I didn't care. But I did. Even as I fought it, I knew I did.

'What were you doing... I saw you bring that girl back here...' I stopped myself, knowing I was coming off as jealous when I had no right to be, and that there was probably a perfectly reasonable explanation.

His eyes studied mine, searching out my hidden meaning. 'Were you worried I was back here fucking her?'

His words stung, and I looked down, unable to respond.

'You can let some random guy put his hands all over you out on the dance floor, and sleep with Professor Gibson but I can't interact with females where I work?' His words were bitter and harsh, but his voice remained calm, too calm, and low, intended for only me to hear. He ran his hands over his face, his frustration evident. 'Christ, Eliza. What do you want from me?' He pressed the heels of his hands into his eyes. 'I'm tired of your head games. You need to figure out what the fuck you want.'

I swallowed down my nerves. 'I know,' I said, though my voice came out breathy and unsure.

He frowned and shook his head. He leaned in toward me, closing me in against the wall, his height causing him to tower over me. 'So what is it then…?'

I didn't know exactly what he was asking, but I had an idea. He was inquiring about us. I looked up into his eyes, and all my resolve softened. 'Cohen, please…' I breathed, barely a whisper and laid my head on his chest.

He pulled me securely to him and held me in place. We didn't say anything for several moments, just stood together, the beating of our hearts thumping in rhythm.

'Ashlyn and Aiden got engaged,' I said, meeting his eyes.

He nodded. 'I knew. He told me he planned to do it.'

'Oh.'

Cohen's brow creased. 'Is that what's got you upset?' His thumb skimmed along my jaw, as if to coax a response from me, but I stayed quiet. 'Eliza… You are a mystery to me.'

I stared up into icy-blue eyes that held so much kindness and beauty in one perfect package. Maybe I was screwed up in the head. I trusted that Cohen wouldn't hurt me, but it was life's circumstances that worried me, and I was pretty sure Cohen wouldn't want me once he found out the truth.

His eyes stayed on mine, looking worried. 'You can't be with me, but you can grind up against some guy out there, huh?' He placed his hands against my shoulders, holding me in place to monitor my reaction.

Watching him look me over, like he was inspecting me for damages was infuriating. I wasn't his to protect, to look over. Then why did a small part of me enjoy the feeling? The way Cohen was always teasing me and his damn nicknames—I'd tried to convince myself that it all grated against my nerves, that I didn't like it… but that was a lie. Maybe I was glutton for pain—I attracted what I couldn't have just to torture myself.

The truth was I felt alive with Cohen. He made the baggage of my past feel lighter, helped me to just live in the moment. It was refreshing. Maybe it was because it didn't seem like there could be any sort of future for us—me with my loose morals and him with his…perfection—that made it so easy for me to spend time around him.

I couldn't help but smile at the curve of his mouth, and the playful grin that urged me on. I thought about the smooth, tanned skin of his shoulders and back, where I longed to dig my nails in and hold on to for dear life. Because I was convinced that was what being with Cohen would be like—a life-altering experience in which I'd need to grasp onto tight and not let go. He wasn't the kind of guy you let get away. That thought popped into my mind, unbidden and unwelcome. But once it was there, I couldn't push it away.

He leaned in slowly and pressed a soft kiss to my lips. 'What do you want from me? Tell me.'

The hallway was empty and dimly lit with bare florescent bulbs every several feet, and even though it wasn't at all private, I wanted him. I gripped his sides, and lifted up to meet his lips again. The height of my heels made it easier to kiss him. 'This. Please.' I didn't even know what I was asking for. All I knew was that I was slightly drunk, and a mix of emotions ranging from sad to horny were racing through my system.

Cohen lowered his mouth to mine and kissed me thoroughly, his tongue pushing past my lips to coax and flirt with mine. All of my senses buzzed with his presence. Cohen alone was intoxicating, forget the alcohol. How in the world had I ever thought that Stu was enough?

He gripped my ass and hauled me closer, pressing me up against the firm length of him, rubbing both hands up and down my behind. I could tell he was already hard, and my body responded. I let out a soft whimper when I felt his thick ridge press against my hip.

He cupped the back of my knee and lifted my thigh, securing it around his hip, and nudged into me. He, above all other men, knew how to make me wet in an instant. Or was it just because of the anticipation of being with him, and the fact we hadn't been intimate yet? I wasn't completely sure, but I knew that it didn't really matter. Before I realized what was happening, Cohen had picked me up and was carrying me down the hall, my high-heel-clad feet bouncing against his backside. He reached a door, unlocked it and brought me inside of what looked to be an office. He locked the door behind us, then set me on my feet and returned to kissing me, pressing my back up against the door, his hands roughly exploring my body.

He tugged the neck of my tank top and the cups of my bra down, freeing my breasts, and bent down to taste them. His mouth and hands were everywhere and I leaned my head back against the door, closing my eyes. All my senses were heightened as I lost myself in his touch, the masculine scent of his skin, the rough stubble on his jaw and his eager kisses.

I opened my eyes to watch him, needing to know that it was really him here with me. My chest rose and fell quickly with each nip and kiss he laid across my breasts. I threaded my fingers through his hair and tugged, holding him closer. 'Cohen,' I moaned.

His fingers fumbled with the button on my jeans, and once it and my zipper were undone, his hand slid along my belly, inside my panties and his warm fingers were inside me, stroking me from the inside out. I was soaking wet, and my body provided no resistance, sucking him in greedily. I cried out when he added a second finger and started pumping harder.

I grabbed his shoulders for support when I felt my legs shaking, and Cohen slowed his pace, lazily fucking me with his fingers, sliding them in inch by delicious inch and then retreating.

I fumbled with his belt buckle and tugged at his jeans. His free hand helped me and together, we yanked down his jeans. Reluctantly pulling his fingers out of my panties, I dropped to my knees in front of him and looked up, my cheek nuzzling into his boxer briefs. He stroked the strands of my hair back from my face and looked down into my eyes.

I slowly pulled his boxers down until his beautiful cock sprang free. I nipped and licked from his balls up to the tip while he buried his hand in my hair. 'Oh, fuck, Eliza,' he moaned, begging for more contact. 'Come here, baby.' He gripped the shaft in his hand and fed it into my mouth, pushing his hips forward with gentle pressure to drive it into my mouth. I clutched his length in both hands, and impatiently pulled him even deeper, swirling my tongue over the head as I sucked. His cock jerked in my mouth and he let out a stream of obscenities.

My panties were soaking wet and my pussy begged to be filled, but still, I continued enthusiastically sucking him. It had never turned me on so much to do this, but Cohen's genuine response was hot. He continued rocking his hips forward, pushing himself farther each time into my mouth until soon his cock was hitting the back of my throat. I gagged once accidentally and he quickly pulled out. 'I'm sorry.' His eyes held mine with a look of confusion and concern. 'I didn't mean to choke you, you're just so fucking good at this, it's hard to hold back with you.' He stroked my cheek in apology.

I smiled up at him with swollen, damp lips. 'It's okay.' I liked that I affected him so much and got him to lose almost all control. I was pretty sure I affected him in ways other girls never had and I liked that, too.

His thumb stroked my bottom lip and I sought out his cock again, licking and suckling the head.

His earpiece crackled with static and he pressed it to his ear, listening to a conversation I couldn't make out.

'Fuck,' he groaned, with frustration rather than pleasure. He hauled me to my feet then tucked himself back inside his pants. 'I've got to go, babe. There's a fight outside.'

The thought of stopping just then was torture. I was about to suggest we meet up in ten minutes in the bathroom, when he pulled me in for a tender kiss.

'Can we finish this later at home, where there's an actual bed and I can take care of you like you deserve?'

I returned his kiss, and without thinking blurted, 'Yes.'

He nodded and kissed my lips softly. 'Thank God. I don't think this thing will go down until I come at least twice.' He winced and adjusted his erection in his pants.

I grinned, loving how worked up I could get him. 'That shouldn't be a problem.'

His fingers skimmed over my belly, lightly tracing my hip bone and sending a ticklish rush straight to my clit. 'What about you? Will you be okay to wait for me? I can't wait to eat that pretty pussy of yours.'

I whimpered and nodded, while clenching my thighs together. Cohen smirked at my response.

Once our clothes were back in place, he helped me to the rest room and set off to the front of the club to deal with the disturbance.

I was shocked by my appearance. My bun was a now a loose wreck of curls thanks to Cohen's roaming hands, and my cheeks were flushed and pink. I finger-combed my hair, choosing to leave it down and went to re-join Ashlyn and Aiden, who were no doubt wondering where I'd disappeared to.

When I got home, I changed out of my jeans and into yoga pants to get more comfortable. I curled up on my couch with my cats and made sure my cell phone ringer was turned up to full volume to wake me in case I fell asleep when Cohen called. I turned the TV on to add some background chatter and settled in to wait.

An hour later, I was still flipping through the channels, waiting for his call, when the shrill sound of my cell ringing startled me. It was Cohen.

Home in 10 min. Up for hanging out?

If hanging out was code for fucking, why yes, yes I was.. Those next ten minutes ticked by more slowly than the entire hour before them, but finally I heard Cohen's SUV rumbling to a stop outside. I locked up and met him on the porch. Still dressed in his black security T-shirt, he looked hot and tough. I liked knowing that even though he had a sweet, soft side to him, he worked as a bouncer at a downtown club and tonight was breaking up a fight. There was actually nothing I didn't like about Cohen and that realization scared me a little bit. He jogged up the porch steps and swept me up into a hug, lifting my bare feet from the ground. He planted a sweet kiss on my temple and lowered me down.

'You want to come up?' he asked.

I nodded, eagerly, and he laughed. 'Good. I just need to grab a shower first. Tonight was insane.'

Once we got upstairs, I lounged on his bed while he headed into the bathroom to clean up. I pulled back the blankets and snuggled into the warm, inviting scent of Cohen that was all over the sheets. I didn't even complain when Bob jumped up to join me, sprawling out across the foot of the bed.

When Cohen returned, dress in only his black boxer briefs, my heart started thudding. I didn't know what might happen between us tonight. The heated passion from earlier had diminished, but not worn away completely. I just wondered now that Cohen could approach things with a clear head, if he'd still want what I needed.

Bob lifted his head at the sound of Cohen's bare feet advancing along the wooden floor, but then he sighed and turned over, making himself more comfortable. Cohen's eyes flicked to mine, and we both smiled.

'This is what you two do when I'm not here, isn't it?' My mouth twitched in a grin.

'No comment.' He lifted Bob off the bed and deposited him in the hallway, closing the door behind him, but not before I heard him softly whisper, 'Sorry buddy,' to the dog.

He crossed the room and joined me on the bed, lying beside me so our faces were only inches apart.

'Hey, beautiful,' he whispered softly.

For the first time, I noticed just how exhausted he looked. His eyes were shadowed by dark circles underneath them, and a few faint lines marred his forehead. I traced a single fingertip along the skin, and he closed his eyes, as if savoring my touch.

I ran my hands along his chest, over the coarse hair and taut muscle. I trailed the back of my fingers over his belly, and gauged his response. His cock wasn't yet hard, for once, but twitched in the snug boxer briefs.

His eyes were still closed, and he had a small smile planted on his lips. 'That feels nice.'

'Turn over. I'll give you a massage.' As soon as the words left my mouth, I sucked in a breath. Memories of giving Paul backrubs flashed back to me. He loved to have his back scratched, and I'd practically leave welts scraping my nails across his skin. But this was different, I reminded myself.

Cohen rolled over and accepted the offer. I rubbed his shoulders, neck and scalp using the pads of my fingers. His breathing slowed and evened out as he relaxed into my touch. I leaned down and looked at him. Closed eyes. Deep breathing. Mouth slack. He was asleep.

I chuckled to myself and curled my body up next to his sleeping form, dragging the blankets up to cover us both. He rolled to his side, and pulled me against his chest. 'Night, Easy E,' he mumbled.

'Night.' I exhaled softly, surprised that the emotion rushing through my system was that of relief. I knew sex would change the dynamic between us, and even though my body ached for that intimacy with Cohen, I hadn't quite decided if that change would be welcome. Things were starting to feel very relationship-ish and I wasn't sure I could go there with him. My last thought before I drifted off to sleep was that I was safe for another day, safe in Cohen's arms.

Chapter 14

Why I'd agreed to a family dinner at Cohen's mom's house, I had no idea. But somehow, the following Saturday, I found myself dressed in a skirt and sweater set trailing dutifully behind Cohen and Bob, with a still-warm casserole dish in my arms.

Denise pulled open the door once we got closer, and Grace burst from inside and into Cohen's waiting arms. She began climbing him like a jungle gym while Denise looked adoringly at her son. It was clear that he was a hero in her eyes.

Bob tugged spastically at the leash, ramming into my legs and causing me to nearly tumble. Thankfully, I remained upright with the casserole still intact.

'Mom, Grace, you remember Eliza, right?'

They both turned and stared as if I were a three-headed monster.

'Why's she here?' Grace asked him, climbing down his lanky frame until her feet were once again on the ground. 'You've never brought a girl with you before.'

Cohen cracked a grin. 'From the mouths of babes.' He placed a reassuring hand on my lower back, and leaned in close to my ear. 'Sorry about that.'

Denise's mouth curved into a stiff smile and she held open the door. 'Please come in.'

I followed her inside and into the kitchen, where I presented her with the casserole dish.

She took it and suspiciously eyed its contents through the glass lid. 'What is it?'

'It's baked brie and cranberries.'

She frowned. 'Oh. Well, thank you.' She held the container out from her body like it was filled with nuclear waste and walked it over to the counter to set it aside.

I'd like to say the evening got better after that, but sadly it didn't. Both mother and daughter clearly adored Cohen and delighted at each thing he did and said, and otherwise pretty much ignored me. The baked brie was mysteriously forgotten in the kitchen when the roasted chicken and potatoes were placed on the table, until I went to retrieve it. I'd been torn about bringing something, but Cohen liked the idea and thought it would be a nice touch.

Cohen took a large serving of the soft cheese and smeared it over a slice of bread, commenting on what a great cook I was as he chewed. This caused his mother's frown to return, and a line to crease her forehead as if to punctuate her opinion of another woman feeding her son.

Cohen, for his part, seemed oblivious that these two ladies in his life did not think there was room for a third, and I wasn't about to point that out to him. That wasn't my intention anyway, was it? So I remained quiet during dinner and watched the easy family banter they shared.

His pager beeped noisily, startling Grace. I always teased him about how loud he kept the volume turned up. He said he didn't want to miss a call. He checked the pager and frowned. A second later, it beeped it again.

Crap. Even I knew the double beep was a bad sign.

He jumped up from where he sat, full of the excited energy that infused him whenever a call came, and shrugged into his jacket.

'You'll be okay?' He leaned down and kissed the top of my head, the same treatment he'd given to his mom and Grace earlier. And of course, it didn't escape his mother's notice.

I nodded my head weakly. 'Of course. Be safe.' For the first time I felt a pang of worry uncoil in my belly. Cohen regularly put himself in harm's way. It wasn't something I wanted to dwell on, so I said a silent prayer, pushed the worry away, and fixed a smile on my face. The realization struck me that him leaving meant I was staying. With his mother. And sister. And Boo Boo. Lord help me.

I helped his mom clear the table and load the dishwasher. We worked side by side in relative silence, but I could tell something was on her mind—more than just Cohen's well-being on his call.

She clutched the casserole dish in her hands, looking down at it thoughtfully. I braced myself for what she might say. 'Cohen's a special young man.'

'I completely agree.' I offered a smile, trying to show her that we were on the same team, and despite what she thought my intention was not to hurt him.

'He's been through a lot in his life. I'm not sure what he's told you, but Grace and I really rely on him, and we...can't have anything changing that.'

Oh-kay. I was basically being told to back off from her son, and that he was going to remain a Mama's boy. 'We're not dating, Denise. We're just friends.' I stood my ground, my voice never wavering.

She nodded, drawing her lips together tightly. 'I know. I can just see that there's something between you. Be careful with him, he's important to us.'

'I understand.' I nodded, taking the dish from her hands and relaxing a little.

Grace came in and tugged on my shirt. 'Can you come play with me? Cohen never plays Barbies.'

Denise smiled at her daughter, her eyes crinkling in the corners, and I noticed that her eyes were the exact same shade of blue as her son. 'Go ahead. I've got this.'

I trailed behind Grace, following her through the tiny house and into her bedroom. The walls were painted cotton-candy pink and an equally cheerful hot-pink bedspread screamed little girl. But the worn carpeting and drafty window warned of a single mother struggling to make ends meet. Toys were scattered haphazardly across the floor, apparently having exploded from a toy chest shoved into the corner. She seemed to know where everything was, though, and led me to the spot where she kept her Barbies. I joined her on the carpet beneath the window and she handed me a deranged looking Barbie that had recently suffered the unfortunate accident of having all her hair cut off at the scalp. We weren't going to be playing Beauty Salon Barbie, it seemed.

I spotted a plastic bag full of doll clothing and pulled it closer. 'All right, Grace. How about we play Shopping Mall and take Barbie to try on some different outfits?'

Grace nodded enthusiastically and I dumped the bag on the floor with a sigh, sorting shirts, pants and dresses into piles. While being with Grace was certainly less stressful than hanging out with Denise, I still prayed that Cohen wouldn't be gone long.

A couple of hours later, a sweaty and worn out Cohen returned to his mother's house to pick me up. His excitement to go on the call had drained away, and had been replaced by somberness at what he'd just seen and experienced. I'd learned not to ask questions, but instead knew that if he wanted to share the details, he would. During the lake house weekend, I'd heard him telling some of the more difficult stories to Aiden. Like the time a car went over the bridge into the Chicago river, and Cohen, being a certified rescue diver, went in after the woman trapped in the vehicle. He'd delivered babies and fought fires and arrived on the scene of fatal accidents more times than he could count in the last few years.

I gave him a reassuring hug, and his expression lifted just a bit, then I went to the kitchen to retrieve my casserole dish. In Cohen's presence, Denise was nothing but polite and friendly, her earlier demeanor gone but not forgotten.

We said our goodbyes and left, since it was past Grace's bedtime already.

I said nothing about his mother attempt to warn me off on the drive home. It was dark outside and the hum of the highway kept Cohen lost in his thoughts, a slight smile playing on his lips.

He had everything he needed in his mother and sister—well, almost everything. I knew he was waiting for the right girl to come into his life. I don't think he realized that the bar was raised too high, that his mother was overbearing and that he just seemed too...perfect.

Regardless, I knew the right girl would be lucky to have him, and acknowledged the fact that in a tiny, unused corner of my heart, I held out hope that girl might be me.

I headed up to my bedroom alone, needing some space from Cohen and the dinner that had stirred up strange sentiments about family and life that I hadn't felt in a while.

I glanced around at what used to be my favorite spot in my beautiful townhome, the window seat in my bedroom that overlooked the back yard. Now that I knew Cohen's bed sat above me in exactly the same spot, I couldn't quite look at it the same way. I trailed my fingers along the champagne-colored fabric I custom-ordered for the seat covering, and the stack of coffee table books I'd neatly arranged there. My fingers skimmed over the spines of the books. I didn't give a crap about Patisseries of Paris, or Dog

Breeds of Westminster, or Buildings of the New York Skyline, I just thought the stack of books looked interesting, intriguing. But instead—much like my life—they were dull and lifeless and without meaning.

I sat on the seat and stared out into the darkness. The past several years of my life tumbled through my brain and I realized that I'd been afraid to graduate from college. To actually begin living my life. I'd hidden in the shelter and routine of student life, like I could pretend his death never happened, knowing I could never again open myself up to that kind of pain. But all I'd succeeded in doing was stunting myself from living. It was no wonder Ashlyn thought Cohen and I were a good match. And we probably were, when you looked at our emotional levels, our maturity. I'd done everything in my power to stop myself from experiencing anything even remotely real. When all I'd succeeded in doing was accumulating a collection of worthless things, and worked my way through more than enough men to fill several little black books. All I felt was empty and hollow.

I moved from the seat to my bed and pulled a throw pillow into my lap. I picked up my cell phone and dialed my mom, deciding that it'd been too long since we'd spoken.

She could tell something was wrong, even though the only words I'd uttered were 'Hi Mom.'

'What's got you all tangled up? How's school?'

'School's fine, Mom.' I let out a slow sigh. 'It's just…I've been thinking lately…about Paul.'

'Oh, Eliza Jane, don't do that to yourself. Dr. Carson told you. None of that was your fault. It's time to move on honey. '

'It's Liz, Mom. *Liz.*'

She huffed softly into the phone. 'That's not your name. That's the cold, hard version of yourself you've tried to become, honey. It's time to get back to being you.'

114

Easier said than done. She'd given me this same talk numerous times, and I knew it was better to keep my mouth shut than try and argue with her. 'There's someone I've sort of been seeing, and his family and relationships are really important to him. I know you think it's time, but I can't seem to get over the hurdle of losing Paul like that and, I mean, look at your and Dad's relationship. It's not exactly a winning endorsement for love and marriage.'

'I'm happy you're seeing someone, honey, but leave it to you to jump fifty steps ahead, into marriage and babies. Just take it one day at a time. And as for your dad and I...you think I regret marrying him?' She chuckled. 'No Eliza, I don't. I got you and your brother out of the deal. Those first fifteen years of marriage were the happiest time in my life. I don't regret them at all. Things eventually changed between me and your dad, and while I wouldn't wish for that to happen to anyone, I wouldn't change a thing.'

I bit my lip, weighing this new information. Hearing my mother, who was once so bitter and jaded about men after her divorce tell me that she'd do it all over again, was shocking. I didn't need a Ph.D. in psychology to realize that I'd been hiding behind my parents' divorce and subsequent falling out as an excuse to avoid commitment in my own life.

It was hard to realize, even though it should have probably set my mind at ease.

'He sounds like a nice guy. I bet Paul would have liked him.' I could hear the smile in her voice.

My heart thudded painfully in my chest, as if to remind me it was still there. 'I've gotta go, Mom. Thanks for the advice.'

I clicked off the phone and tossed it on my bed.

Maybe I should just come clean with Cohen. But no, I knew I couldn't do that. Once he learned the real truth about me, he wouldn't want me anymore. I wouldn't be able to live up to his ridiculously high expectations. I wasn't perfect. Not even close.

If he really felt something for me—he'd have to prove it. It might be deceitful to test him this way—to see how far he was willing to go—but I needed this. I need him to show me I was worth risking everything for. To put his money where his mouth was and make me his.

How could I return his sentiment by risking my heart, if he wasn't willing to risk his body? There was only one solution. I needed to seduce Cohen once and for all, and then I would see where we stood. Now that I'd made this decision, my belly danced with nerves. Could I really go through with this? And everything it might mean?

I had to. I had to know how Cohen really felt about me. And how I would respond to him in turn.

Chapter 15

Despite all the crazy self-talk running through my mind all day, I knew what I needed to do. It was time to put my big girl panties on and deal. The talk with my mom the night before weighed on me. For five years I'd protected my heart like it was my damn job, because I'd seen firsthand how easily it could all be ripped away from you. And though I wasn't ready to put it all on the line just yet, I knew I needed to open myself up to Cohen more than I had thus far.

I hoisted the brown paper sack I was holding onto my hip as I knocked on his door.

Cohen stood before me, looking solemn in worn jeans, a white T-shirt and bare feet. 'Hey, come in.' He pulled the door open wider. 'Are you back, Easy E?' His words were full of deeper meaning, and I gave a brief nod.

'With a peace offering.' I held up the bag, filled with cartons of Chinese food and a six-pack of imported beer that I knew was his favorite.

He smiled, a big, genuine grin that showed his perfectly straight white teeth and hit me full force just how gorgeous this man was. 'Thank God. I'm tired of sleeping with that damn dog. And with you back, I don't feel bad kicking him out of my bed.'

I laughed and crossed the threshold to his apartment. 'Don't get ahead of yourself, I didn't say I was staying the night.' But I knew I would. I'd missed Cohen something fierce. I busied myself in the kitchen, loading up two plates with the Chinese food when he came up behind me and wound his arms around my waist, caging me in against the counter. I felt his warm breath tickle the back of my neck.

'Don't tease me, Eliza. You come over here, bearing food and beer and offering yourself up to me…don't expect me to not take what you're offering.'

What was I offering? Had I really thought this through? What did Cohen think my being here meant, exactly? He brushed his nose along the back of my neck, inhaling my scent. 'You don't understand the effect you have on me,' he whispered.

I swallowed and turned in his arms so I was facing him, and looked up to meet his eyes. Without my heels I felt miniature against him, barely clearing his chin. He lowered his mouth to mine, but he didn't kiss me right away like I expected.

'Why are you here? What do you want?' he whispered against my lips.

'Everything,' I blurted without thinking.

His mouth claimed mine in a passionate kiss, his lips moving against my own as his tongue swept inside. I eagerly matched his kiss, swirling my tongue with his in a dance that was anything but delicate. He suckled my bottom lip and bit at the soft flesh. The sting of pain was unexpected and hot, and I let out a soft whimper.

He pulled back and met my eyes. 'Is that what you need? For me to take control? You need me to be rough?' he breathed, his voice deep and coarse. His large hands framed my face and rather indelicately he forced my chin up, gripping my jaw and neck. 'Is that what I need to do to get through to you?'

I squeaked out a response as he knitted his hands underneath my hair and gently pulled so my head tipped back and he could take my mouth again.

I liked this side of Cohen, this strong man I knew was in there the whole time. I liked not having to think for a change, and my brain reveled in the emptiness that followed. I turned over all rational thought and logic to the moment and just felt. Cohen. And everything he had to offer.

I leaned into him, hungry for more contact and loving the feel of the length of his firm body pressed against mine. There was only one way to test how he really felt about me—and, I supposed, how I really felt about him too. I didn't know why it'd taken me so long to realize what the solution to all this Cohen-obsessing was. He wouldn't be out of my system until we slept together.

New plan.

I needed to face my fears and make him face his. Was he really willing to make me his? And perhaps more importantly, was I willing to make him mine?

His hands began fumbling at the hem of my shirt, and I raised my arms to allow him to lift it above my head. I stood before him topless, since I'd taken off my bra for the night.

I straightened my shoulders, pushing out my breasts for his inspection.

It was obvious how much he enjoyed my tits. His hands and mouth began to stroke them, caress, kiss and nibble almost as if he was on autopilot, drawn in by some powerful homing device guiding him to his objective.

I loved how thoroughly he worshipped my body. He feasted on my flesh until I was flushed and warm. I tugged gently on his hair to pull him back up to kiss me. His tongue savagely invaded my mouth, stroking mine while his hips gently rocked forward, bumping his tense erection against my belly. My hips automatically flexed towards his, seeking, wanting.

I dropped my knees, needing to taste him. As I settled to the floor between his feet, his hands were already at his waistband, working to free himself from his jeans. I looked up at him and held his gaze while he offered me a taste. I remained still, mouth open, hands on his thighs as he gripped his shaft and began working himself in and out of my mouth, watching as I swirled my tongue along the swollen head.

'Fuck, babe.' He gripped my hair, pushing himself farther into my mouth. 'Just like that.'

I enthusiastically took him deeper, opening as wide as I could to accept him. I bobbed up and down the length of him, feasting greedily on every thick inch of his manly goodness, unable to help the damp noises my mouth made against his flesh or the little groans of desire when he bumped the back of my throat.

A second later, he placed his hands underneath my arms and hauled me roughly to my feet. 'In my bed. Now.' His fingers on the base of my spine prodded me forward, toward his bedroom.

I was only too happy to oblige, being insanely horny and just as curious about exactly how far he was going to let this go.

When we entered his room he kept the light switched off, and turned me to face him. He bent and tasted my left breast, and then my right, nibbling my skin before he rose. He unbuttoned my jeans. 'Take these off,' he commanded. 'The panties too.'

He had to know what he was asking. The last time we'd been together I'd made it clear that my underwear needed to stay on, otherwise there were no promises of me staying off his cock.

I removed my jeans, and then slowly, carefully slid my panties down my legs. It didn't escape my notice that I happened to be wearing the white cotton undies I'd joked with Ashlyn were my most virginal pair.

Cohen's eyes moved along my legs, watching me drop the panties to my ankles and fling them off with my toe. He swallowed, and in the shadowy room, I could see his Adam's apple bob in his throat.

Butterflies—no, more like a flock of birds, large birds, like peacocks, or ostriches—rioted in my belly. I hadn't been this nervous when I'd lost my own virginity. I wasn't positive that was what we were going to do, until I noticed the air in the room felt different and Cohen's gaze more needy, and I knew that sex was on the menu.

'Come here.' He held out his hand and I took it, letting him lead me to the bed.

We collided together in the center of the mattress, a tangle of arms and legs as we kissed roughly for several minutes. I wasn't sure if I should take matters into my own hands, as the more experienced one, or allow Cohen to lead so I could be sure this was what he wanted. I chose the latter.

After several minutes, he shifted and hauled me with him. 'I don't have any condoms,' he breathed against my neck.

Holy shit! Were we really going to do this? 'I think I have one in my purse,' I heard myself saying.

'Which is where?'

'In my apartment.' I grinned, guiltily. Surely this would be the breather we needed to calm the situation, for him to get back under control.

Cohen stood and pulled on a pair of jogging shorts from the floor, sans boxers, and I giggled at the sight of him.

'What?' he looked down, and chuckled himself. His erection caused the shorts to tent out in the front, making it extremely obvious he was sporting some serious wood. 'It's dark. No one will see anything,' he assured me.

'Yeah, but if they do, they'll call the police.'

He laughed again, and left the bedroom.

'My purse is on the island,' I called to his retreating backside.

The entire time he was gone, my mind alternated between panic and euphoria, and my heart slammed against my chest at the flurry of emotion.

He returned a minute later with my entire purse, the large bulge still protruding out of the front of his shorts. He dropped them to his ankles and joined me on the bed once again.

I removed the condom and set my purse on the floor. The plastic package crinkled in my hands, the noise splintering the silence of the room. I checked Cohen's expression for doubt, for any sign he didn't want this and found none.

'Yes?' Somehow, verbal agreement seemed to also be in order. A decision like this wasn't supposed to be taken lightly.

'Yes.' Cohen's voice was low, but strong.

I tore open the package, then leaned toward him and placed the condom on his belly. He unrolled it onto himself while we kissed. It seemed to be taking an inordinate amount of time, but I didn't want to embarrass him by questioning if he knew what he was doing.

Once his hands came up and cupped my jaw, I knew it was on and there was nothing stopping us. My heartbeat built to an uncomfortable level, but still I waited to see what his next move would be.

I heard him gasp, and I opened my eyes. He looked uncomfortable and his erection had softened slightly. 'Fuck, this thing is tight.' I bit back a laugh, because of course it was supposed to be tight, but when I looked down and saw it actually appeared to be cutting off his circulation and only covered half his length, my laughter died on my lips.

'Cohen, we don't need it.' I'd been tested recently and up until this point had always used condoms, despite being on the pill.

He pulled the rubber free with a snap and tossed it to the floor beside the bed.

If it was any other guy, I'd think it was a plot to go condom-free, but not Cohen, I could tell it had truly surprised him how uncomfortable the offending piece of latex had been.

'Better?' I whispered.

He nodded lightly. 'Much.' He gripped my upper arms and hauled me onto his lap. 'Now come here.'

We began kissing again as I moved against his hips. This time when his shaft slid up and down my wet folds, it was without any barrier between us.

I waited for him to stop me, to say something—anything. But he remained quiet aside from his rough breathing and the occasional groan. When I felt him begin to slide inside me, I don't know which of us was more surprised, but there was no denying it felt right. It felt better than right, it was perfect. He sunk into me slowly, inch by inch, until he was fully buried in my warm heat. He let out a groan and a string of incoherent curse words.

This beautiful man was giving me something precious to him, claiming me as his with each thrust of his hips, with each breath and kiss that we shared. The thought made me dizzy and light-headed, and made my limbs tremble, and then Cohen thrust into me and swept away all coherent thought.

I'd thought at first that having me on top meant I'd do all the work, but Cohen held my hips firmly in place while he pushed upward, rocking his hips against me at a steady pace. I placed my hands on his chest and watched his expression and his icy blue eyes turn dark with desire.

I felt too exposed on top like this, not that the position was new or anything, but with Cohen, it felt like something more. He watched my movements—and not just the way my chest bounced—but he also looked deep into my eyes, watching my every expression. I gripped his perfectly formed pectorals as he continued to drive into me, his features alight with wonder and passion.

I had no idea how long he would last, since I hadn't had sex with a virgin since I was a teenager—and of that experience I remembered exactly two things: the excruciating pain, like I was being penetrated with a knife, and that Tyler Simonson had lasted exactly forty-nine seconds (I'd counted). But Cohen surprised me by pumping into me at a steady pace for much longer than I expected. And when he hauled me off his lap suddenly, I thought maybe he was going to come, but instead he positioned himself over me, spread my thighs apart with both hands, pressed into me again and admired the spot where our bodies joined.

His thrusts grew harder, and I bit my lip from crying out. His breathing became uneven and erratic as he struggled to maintain control. 'Oh fuck, fuck, baby,' he groaned. 'You feel amazing.'

I loved that Cohen didn't hold back with me. I grasped his forearms, which were still holding my thighs spread apart. I could feel his muscles tense from trying not to come too soon. 'Cohen,' I moaned as my own orgasm built.

His eyes flicked to mine, a slow, sexy smile curving his mouth. 'Tell me what to do…what you like…' he whispered against my lips, kissing me softly.

'Fuck me harder,' I breathed. I was already so close.

He grunted and his thrusts grew more fierce, shorter drives that pummeled into me and shook the bed.

I whimpered. My hands slid from his back down to his ass, and I gripped him tighter to me. 'Don't stop. Just like that.'

His fingers tightened on my thighs, biting into the tender flesh as he drove into me.

I arched my back and cried out his name as a powerful orgasm ripped through me. Cohen slowed his movements, somehow knowing exactly what I needed. He watched as a lazy smile crossed my lips. I could feel my inner walls pulsing around him in the aftereffects of my orgasm.

Recognition changed his expression, and I could tell he felt the gentle squeezes too.

'Fuck, Eliza.'

I pulled him down on top of me and kissed him passionately as his breathing quickened. His kisses were disjointed and halting, like he was struggling to concentrate on everything at once. He wasn't annoying and loud like some of the men I'd been with. He bit his lip to keep from moaning out, but that didn't stop the gasps of air from coming hot against my neck as he struggled to maintain control. It was freaking hot.

He continued his steady thrusts against me as I wrapped my arms around him and held him to me. 'I'm going to come, babe,' he whispered.

'Inside me,' I murmured.

His body shook with his release, and I held him tighter, clutching him to my chest as a low moan escaped from his throat.

He buried his face into my neck as I felt his warm semen flood inside me.

I exhaled quietly, satisfied and content and yet terrified, and knew that nothing would be the same again.

Chapter 16

The second time we had sex that night the experience was slower, more controlled. There was a marked difference. It was making love. Cohen ensured every part of my body was aching and ready for him before he took me. He moved slowly above me, his eyes locked on mine as I gripped his biceps. He whispered my name softly next to my ear, as if to demonstrate what this meant to him. It was clear our first time was for me—rougher, more intense—and this second time it for was for him, tender, careful, savoring.

No words needed to be said, it was obvious what he was telling me. In every touch, every kiss, I knew exactly what he was saying, but the full reality hit me when we finished, and he folded me into his arms and held me tightly against him. That scared me more than his willingness to give me his virginity.

After, Cohen suggested we take a shower together. It would be another first for him—showering with a woman—he'd said, but I'd refused, needing some space from him and the intensity of the moment.

He allowed me to shower first, and I took my time under the warm spray of water, vigorously scrubbing away all traces of his aftershave from my skin. Once I was thoroughly pink, I emerged from the shower to find a set of pajamas laid out for me on his bed—a large white T-shirt and a pair of his black boxer briefs.

When I wandered into the living room to find him, he was settled on the couch with a sleepy Bob lying at his feet. I stepped over Bob and sat down next to him.

'Mmm. Warm beer and cold Chinese food, my favorite,' he joked, setting a plate in front of me, and arranging various cartons on the coffee table.

I laughed, happy to see that despite the weight of what we'd just done, it was still just Cohen and me. I'd completely forgotten about the provisions I'd brought over being left out on the counter while we were occupied in the bedroom.

I speared a piece of the sesame chicken, opting for a fork instead of the chopsticks and took a bite. Despite being room temperature, the food tasted amazing. I balanced the plate on my knees and reflected on how thankful I was for Cohen, for this. I didn't know what the future might hold, and I *so* wasn't ready to go there, but it felt good to be here with him, dressed in his clothes, enjoying a nice evening in.

Cohen opened my bottle of beer and set it before me. 'For you, beautiful.'

'Thanks, sexy.'

He grinned and caught my eye. 'How was everything…for you?' His head tipped towards his bedroom door, and I knew he was asking about his performance.

'You're kidding right? If screaming your name and having two orgasms didn't clue you in, let me assure you, you did just fine, sweetheart.' I patted the top of his head.

He chuckled, and took a swig of his own beer. 'What the fuck were those, by the way? Micro-mini condoms?' he teased.

I rolled my eyes, knowing he wanted to hear me say that he was exceptionally large. 'It was a regular-size condom, Cohen.' I mentally made a note that he'd need the large-sized condoms for next time. Or I was fine using none at all.

'Hm,' he thoughtfully tapped a fingertip against my lips.

He was bigger than average, but of course I wouldn't tell him that. It was obvious he was feeling pretty damn smug at the moment, and I loved the spark in his baby-blue eyes.

We continued nibbling on the Chinese food, sharing bites of each dish straight from the cartons for several minutes, eating in a comfortable silence.

'So what do you want to do when you graduate next year?' he asked.

I swallowed down the bite of egg roll, wondering if his question was as innocent as it seemed, or if it was laced with speculation on the future—our future—as I'd feared all along. I wasn't ready to come clean with him just yet. Baby steps. 'Um, I don't know. I hope to teach at a university and continue my research. What about you?'

'Definitely staying in Chicago near my mom and sister, getting a good-paying job and hopefully settling down with the right girl. Bob here isn't going anywhere, either,' he rubbed the dog's back. 'And eventually a family of my own, too.'

My heart jumped at the mention of a family and I roughly swallowed down a mouthful of food that had somehow transformed into a tasteless lump in my mouth.

Wordlessly I retired to bed a short while later, and slept soundly nestled into the sheets that smelled of Cohen and our sweaty sexcapades.

Chapter 17

My plan had backfired on me. I wasn't sure if I'd been trying to call his bluff, or just playing a cruel game of chicken with his heart, but Cohen hadn't backed down. He'd raised the stakes—considerably—by giving himself to me, along with his heart on a platter.

I released a frustrated sigh and scrubbed my hands across my face, curling into a pathetic ball on my couch. I should have realized the significance. I should have stopped him. But of course, in that moment, I couldn't have stopped even if I'd wanted to. My brain hadn't been working clearly, and the responses he provoked from my body boggled even me. I never had multiple orgasms. Ever. As in not once. But leave it to sweet, inexperienced Cohen to milk every ounce of pleasure he could from my body. I was starting to become convinced this was some kind of conspiracy. He used my own body against me.

Over the past several years I'd rebuilt myself from the ground up, not stopping until a full personality makeover was complete. And somehow the other night I'd spent with Cohen had unraveled some of my work. Whereas Eliza had preferred tea, Liz became a coffee connoisseur. Eliza always wore flats, Liz purchased a killer selection of heels and learned to walk in them without stumbling—much. Eliza was loving and devoted, Liz lived for fun, no attachments and keeping things casual.

I'd been acting like this whole other person for so long, even I hardly remembered the small town girl I'd been. And Ashlyn had certainly never met her. But somehow Cohen sensed she was still inside me, even insisting on calling me Eliza, which was odd.

I heard the doorbell and my stomach dropped. There was no hiding my tear-streaked face and red, puffy eyes. *Crap*. I pulled open the door and met Ashlyn's worried gaze.

'Lizzie,' she squeaked, pushing in past me. 'What's the matter? You missed our coffee date.' She lifted the large iced Americano she was holding for me.

'Thanks,' I mumbled, half-heartedly. For once not even coffee sounded good.

I waved at her to follow me inside and into the living room, where I collapsed onto the couch. My townhouse was a mess. Though it was nothing like Ashlyn's crazy version of house-keeping, for me, it was a wreck—used tissues littered the coffee table, cold mugs of tea sat untouched and several pieces of mail and a couple of magazines lay scattered on the floor. I'd seen Cohen outside jogging with Bob, and I'd grabbed my mail and scampered back into the house, fumbling and dropping the items at my feet. My heart had alternated between thundering in my chest and clenching in pain—especially when he hadn't come after me.

Not that I'd really been expecting him to, I guess. That was two days ago now, and I still didn't know what to say to him.

After that blissful night with him, I'd left early the following morning while he was still asleep and hadn't returned his calls in the days that followed. I knew it was shitty of me, but I needed to get my head on straight. It felt like everything was collapsing around me, and if and when I told Cohen the truth about me, I didn't know if I could handle his rejection.

'What's wrong? Boy troubles?' Ashlyn asked, settling into an oversized armchair.

'Something like that,' I mumbled and curled my feet up onto the seat underneath me.

'Are you still seeing Stu?' Her face was a mask of worry. Crease lines etched into her forehead as she leaned forward and studied me.

'God, no. I've been done with him for a while.' Gross. I couldn't believe she thought I'd be this upset over Stu. I hadn't even thought about him in weeks.

She moved to sit beside me on the couch and rubbed my back, soothingly. 'Then what is it, sweetie? It's not like you to get so upset.'

I cleared my throat, and wiped both cheeks with my sleeves. 'It's Cohen. We had sex.' *Twice.*

Ashlyn's breath left her chest in a rush. 'Oh crap. And? Was it horrible? Awkward?'

'Oh God, no. Nothing like that. It was better than I could have ever imagined.' I'd set my expectations low, never imagining Cohen would be as naturally gifted as he was.

She raised her eyebrows, impressed. 'So are you guys together now?'

That was the problem. I didn't know how to face Cohen now, how to say what I needed to say. 'There's something I've never told you.'

'What is it, Liz? You know you can tell me anything.'

I nodded slowly, somberly and mumbled that I'd be right back. I didn't need to tell her so much as I needed to show her. Only this would explain why my feelings for Cohen terrified me.

I went into my bedroom and came back carrying an ornate silver box engraved with the word *Love*. I realized for the first time that keeping my love boxed up was more than just a metaphor. I set the box on her lap and then sat down next to her.

'What's this?'

'Open it.'

Ashlyn lifted the lid and looked quizzically down inside at the velvet lining. She lifted the simple gold ring and held it up to the light. 'It's beautiful, but I don't understand.'

I pulled a shaky breath into my lungs, fighting down emotion I thought I'd buried completely. 'I was engaged once.'

Ashlyn's stunned silence betrayed her hurt feelings that I'd kept this from her.

I'd wanted to tell her before, all the times she'd laughed at how carefree I was, or scoffed about me being a commitment-phobe. It'd been on my mind countless times, I just never knew quite what to say. And of course it'd been on my mind the night she'd thrust her large, sparkling diamond ring in my face.

'I was twenty.' I smiled lightly at the memory. 'I was a sophomore in college and trust me, I'd never intended to get engaged so young. But then you never got to meet Paul.'

She watched me, her expression one of concern.

'He was perfect, Ash. Beyond perfect. He was two years older than me. I met him when I was seventeen—he was a busboy at my parent's country club, and definitely not good enough to date their daughter as far as they were concerned. But he won them over eventually. He was sweet, and kind and well-mannered. He'd help my mom clear the dishes after dinner and could talk sports with my dad. He was my first…everything.'

I cleared my throat, realizing I'd gotten a little lost in my own story. I could still see Paul's crooked smile the first time he showed me the cursive *E* he'd had tattooed over his heart. Paul was the reason I started going by Liz. But that was later, of course. After.

'He was driving in from Des Moines, coming to visit me at college for the weekend.'

Ashlyn nestled the ring back into the box and reached over, placing her hand on my knee. 'Liz?'

'It's okay.' I gripped my hands together in my lap, bracing myself for this next part. 'He fell asleep behind the wheel and collided head on with a semi-truck. He was killed instantly.' Because of me. Because of love, I add in my head. Ashlyn would try and talk me out of that notion because that was what she was supposed to do. But I knew. Just like I knew in my heart I was falling for Cohen and I wasn't supposed to. He was off limits for so many reasons, it should have been illegal.

I didn't tell her about the six months after his death when I could barely function, or the two years after that I lived like a zombie, reliant on anti-depressants just to get through each day. My move to Chicago was my chance to start over. I became Liz—hardened, invincible party girl extraordinaire, only looking for a good time and an occasional fling.

There was no way I could have gone on living in Iowa after Paul died. Traces of him were all over the small town where I grew up. Having to pass by my parents' country club where we'd met, restaurants we'd eaten at, or other familiar places on a daily basis would have been too much. I'd taken a semester off school after his death and then transferred to Chicago after that.

I loved living in Chicago now. The hustle and bustle, the pace of it all, the traffic jams and ethnic diversity ensured that I was rarely reminded of my small-town Iowa upbringing.

'Why didn't you ever tell me, Liz?' Ashlyn's concerned voice pulled me from my own thoughts.

'I don't like talking about it—for obvious reasons.'

She nodded and patted my knee again. 'You never judged me for being with Aiden.' She squinted her eyes. 'Well, maybe just a little, but that's only because you're a good friend, and that was kind of freaking crazy of me. But my point is that you've also been there for me. You always had my back, and even if I didn't want to hear what you had to say—you told me. Because that's what friends do.'

This little speech was so unlike Ashlyn, I couldn't help myself for leaning in towards her, studying her like a science experiment.

'You have feelings for Cohen,' she continued. 'Real feelings. And I know you don't want to, but you need to let yourself properly grieve Paul and move on, knowing that he'd want you to be happy. If he was as great as you say, he'd probably even like you ending up with a guy like Cohen.'

Realization slammed into my chest. She was right. How did I not see that before? It came at me with a rush of stunning clarity. Paul would hate what I'd been doing. Too much wine and too much attitude. One night stands. Nameless guys for the sake of forgetting. I cringed when I thought about my affair with Stu.

Crap. Ashlyn was right. Too bad it wasn't going to be that simple.

'Go see him, sweetie. Talk to him, let him in.'

'There's something else though.' I looked down, fidgeting nervously with the throw pillow on my lap.

I took the box from her hands and lifted the velvet lining from the bottom. I hadn't opened this box in many years, but still my fingers knew the exact corner to lift to ease the fabric away. I freed the photograph nestled at the bottom of the box and handed it to Ashlyn.

She studied it with a crinkled brow before speaking. 'This is an ultrasound photo.' Her hand flew to her mouth. 'Oh, Liz.' She flung her arms around me, squeezing me tight, letting me weep softly into her hair.

'I was sixteen weeks along when I lost Paul, and then a week later, I lost the baby too.' I swallowed the lump in my throat, then took the picture from her and returned it to the box, safely tucking it underneath the velvet fabric. 'He'd been hoping for a little girl—he wanted her to look exactly like me.' The memory brought a small smile to my lips. I couldn't believe it'd been five years since I'd been pregnant. I could still remember the exact way

I felt—terrified and then overjoyed all in the blink of an eye. I remembered Paul's eyes turning misty when I told him the news, and him crushing me to his body in a hug before quickly pulling away to be sure he didn't squeeze me too tight and hurt the baby. I recalled the achy soreness in my breasts, the nausea that lasted all day, and my cravings for high protein foods like steak that I'd never been fond of before.

'Liz?' Ashlyn interrupted my private stroll down memory lane. I'd been swept away again, but I knew I needed to finish the story.

'I had to undergo a procedure…and they discovered…' I stopped myself and took a deep breath, my voice growing shaky. 'My body couldn't handle the shock of losing Paul. So not only did I lose him, and then the baby, but I lost my ability to carry another baby, too.'

'Oh honey.' She stroked my hair back from my face lovingly.

'That's why I didn't waste my time on nice guys who would want more. I don't have that in me to give to someone again—figuratively and literally.'

'Shh,' she shushed me, brushing her fingers through my hair.

'Cohen will want a family someday. And a wife with a functioning uterus.' I bit my lip. 'I thought going for the younger guys—the undergrads—was safe. They're not usually thinking ahead about that kind of stuff. But leave it to me to attract the world's most perfect male and have him turn out to be all responsible and focused on his future Mrs. Right.' I rolled my eyes, trying to lighten the situation.

Ashlyn remained quiet, her expression thoughtful.

I carried the box back to my bedroom and instead of hiding it in my closet, where I usually kept it, I set it on my night table. I patted the top of it before going back to Ashlyn. I was glad I had told her, even if it had been hard to talk through. I grabbed some tissues and returned to the living room.

Ashlyn was still on the sofa, her legs tucked underneath her, and her face serious. 'I know you feel something for him. And Cohen has surprised us both at every turn. Maybe he'll surprise you again. I know that he feels strongly for you. Give him a chance, Liz.'

After a deep sigh, I nodded my acquiescence. It felt like a weight had been lifted from my chest, having exposed this dark secret about myself.

'Get yourself cleaned up, honey. You can do this.' She kissed my forehead and then was gone.

I began by cleaning my house. I sorted through the mail, picked up the dishes and trash, dusted the living room, and vacuumed and scrubbed both toilets. After working off some of my nervous energy, I took a long, leisurely shower.

I tied my silk robe loosely around myself while I dried my hair, and then took my time applying my makeup.

I had to hope that not only would Cohen accept my fear of love and inability to have children, but also forgive me for walking out on him. After a few more swipes of mascara and a quick comb of my thick, unruly waves, I was ready. There was no putting it off any longer.

I dressed simply in jeans and a long-sleeved T-shirt, and glanced in the mirror one last time. My eyes were wide with fear and I rolled my shoulders trying to relax.

I focused on my breathing with each step towards Cohen's apartment. Tension coiled in my belly as I stood in front of his door. Before I could talk myself out of it, I made a fist and knocked. I had no clue what I would say…how I would begin the conversation, and prayed that the right words would come to me.

I continued waiting a few moments longer then rapped again, not sure if he heard me the first time. Or maybe he wasn't home. I peeked over the ledge of the balcony to see if his Jeep was parked in the street. It was nowhere in sight, which didn't mean much, considering that parking was insane in this neighborhood, and he'd often park several blocks away just to find a spot.

After waiting another minute, I gave up and walked back downstairs, hoping I wouldn't lose my nerve when he got home.

Chapter 18

I'd fallen asleep on the couch, curled up with Sugar and Honey Bear against my chest. I liked how my cats could tell when I was down and did their part to cheer me up.

Unsure of the time, I reached for my phone and discovered it was three in the morning. It was a second before I realized what had woken me—Bob's insistent barking from upstairs. That was strange. I'd never heard that dog bark. Not ever. And certainly not in the middle of the night. Why wasn't Cohen quieting him down? He was bound to wake up the whole damn neighborhood if he kept that up. Unless he wasn't home.

That thought left me unsettled. Cohen rarely stayed out late, even the times I'd known him to go out with friends. I swallowed down a sharp lump that had suddenly lodged itself in my throat. He was likely out on a call. I never really worried about him going out on calls, the pager made me more annoyed than anything else, but tonight, something felt different.

I slipped on my shoes and headed up to Cohen's door. Bob's barking became louder as I got closer. It was as though he was standing on the other side of the door, wanting to be let out. I pinched the bridge of my nose, trying to think. Had Cohen not been home all day to let the poor creature out? I knocked on the door and waited, but surely if Cohen was home, Bob wouldn't be barking like he was. Of course, there was no answer.

My heart rate sped up while I considered what to do. I tried talking to Bob through the door, assuring him that everything would be okay, but even I wasn't so sure. The night had taken on an eerie quality, and I made my way back downstairs, wanting to be safely inside my apartment and away from the ear-splitting barking that was adding to my stress levels.

I shucked off my shoes and begin pacing the length of my living room. I considered calling Ashlyn and Aiden, but really what could they do? I wondered if Aiden was good at picking locks. Or maybe I could just break down the door.

I picked up my cell phone again to check the time when I noticed a missed call from my landlord, from just a few minutes ago.

That was strange. Why would he call in the middle of the night? Unless someone in the neighborhood had called him about the dog barking his head off in one of his tenant's places.

I dialed his number and waited, the sinking feeling that something was very wrong intensifying as it rang.

This night was strangely reminiscent of the first night I'd met Cohen—waking at three a.m. only to be terrified by a bat. Of course Cohen's calming presence had affected me from that very first night—and I smirked as I remembered eating pancakes in the diner with him.

My landlord picked up on the fourth ring, 'Yeah.'

'Hi, um, it's Liz…you called me.'

'Oh, Liz, good—you're up. Listen, I'm sorry to call so late, but there's been an accident.'

My legs no longer worked properly and I fell backwards onto the couch, landing with a thump as my butt hit the cushion.

'It's the tenant upstairs—Cohen. He's been admitted to Mercy—he's in surgery now. I didn't realize he was a firefighter. Anyway,

I've talked to his mother, and she reminded me that he has a dog that will need taking care of.' He cleared his throat. 'Boo Boo, I think she said he was called.'

'Bob,' I corrected.

'Okay, so can you take care of him until they can get something else figured out?'

'Forget the damn dog—how's Cohen?' The panic in my voice startled even me, as I pleaded silently that he was okay. I realized my landlord had no way of knowing the extent of our relationship.

'All I know is that he fell through the floor in a burning building, he was rushed to the hospital and is undergoing emergency surgery.'

And then he was back to talking about the dog, and making arrangements to give me a key to Cohen's place, but I sagged with relief against the back of the couch. I turned the phone away from my ear and bit my fist, fighting back a cry. This was all too similar to the call I got about Paul all those years ago. But Cohen was still alive, and I prayed he was going to be okay. I repeated the mantra in my head.

'So can you... I mean take the dog out, feed it, stuff like that?'

'Sure.' I replied.

He said he'd be by with the key in a few minutes, so I quickly changed into jeans, and threw on Cohen's Chicago Fire Department sweatshirt over my top.

As soon as Bob had been out to do his business, I hopped in my seldom-used car and I high-tailed it to the hospital to be there when Cohen woke up, praying the entire time that he would be okay.

After parking outside the ER, I jogged into the hospital reception area, boggled by all the signs I saw. I settled for approaching the information desk to inquire about Cohen's whereabouts.

'Are you family?' a frowning middle-aged nurse asked me wearily.

'I'm his...' *Friend? Neighbor?* 'Girlfriend.'

She frowned and shook her head. 'Sorry, family only sweetheart. You'll have to wait over there.' She pointed to a cheerless waiting area behind me, complete with upholstered chairs, carpeting and wallpaper all in the same annoyingly cheerful pastel pattern.

I stalked away into the waiting room, and sank into a chair to wait. A pain above my left eye throbbed and I pressed my palm to my temple, applying pressure to squelch the pain.

I was surprised that I didn't see his mother Denise. I was sure she'd be a wreck. Unless there was a family-only waiting room. It probably had plush chairs, and magazines from this decade. And coffee. I was ready to kill someone for a cup of coffee.

I tuned out the squeak of shoes against the tile floors and the hum of mechanical equipment, along with beeping pagers that remind me of Cohen. I sat for an hour with my head in my heads, reflecting on all that could have been, and all I might have already lost, praying that Cohen would be okay and that he'd give me another chance.

I drifted in and out of consciousness as I played through various scenarios where Cohen was fine and I was completely forgiven, to Cohen crippled for life and angry and bitter towards me. I would probably deserve that treatment for walking out on him the way I did, but he didn't deserve to be hurt. I just prayed that he'd recover from this accident. The rest I could take.

Hushed voices drifted in from the nearby hallway, and I mostly tuned them out until I heard the name Cohen.

I rushed out of the waiting room to find two doctors retreating into the distance, and a nurse standing in the middle of the hall with a file full of paperwork.

'Excuse me, but did I overhear you talking about Cohen? Can you tell me how he is?'

She surveyed me up and down, as if deciding whether she should respond. 'Are you a relative of his?'

Were they all trained to ask that? 'Close enough. I'm the only one who's here for him right now.'

'He's been in surgery for two hours. His mother has been contacted, but my understanding is that she's trying to find someone to stay with the younger sibling so she can get here.'

'I can do it.' The words flew from my mouth before I could even process them.

The nurse looked at me quizzically. 'Okay.' She narrowed her eyes at me then flipped through the file. 'Other than that, we don't know much. He did extensive damage to his shoulder, and is still in surgery.'

I nodded, and shouted 'Thanks,' before scurrying away down the hall.

It was only by a sheer miracle that I found Cohen's mother's house. I was a terrible driver and horrid with directions since I rarely drove, but somehow divine intervention saw to it that I arrived. I stopped my Honda against the curb and approached the house. It was dark and chilly, but the porch light was on, which was promising.

I tapped softly on the door, aware that Grace was probably asleep. A second later, the door opened and a puffy-eyed Denise stood before me.

'Eliza?' she asked.

I nodded. 'Hi. I heard what happened. Can I come in?'

Her eyes darted down to the Chicago Fire Department sweatshirt I was wearing, and a flash of recognition crossed her features. 'Sure.' She held the door open, and I passed by her.

'Our landlord called to ask me to take care of Bob, which I did, by the way. And then I went to the hospital, but they wouldn't tell me anything, because I'm not family.'

Her chin lifted at this and she crossed her arms. 'Haven't you done enough?'

Her tone was sharp, and completely unexpected. I'd just driven halfway across town in the middle of the night because I was worried sick about Cohen. 'Excuse me?'

'Cohen, that's what I'm talking about. Before the accident, he'd been distracted and moping, quite unlike himself the past few days. He said you'd stopped speaking to him suddenly and he didn't understand why.'

I sunk to the sofa at the weight of her words. I had caused another accident. First Paul, now Cohen. The weight of all my mistakes rushed back to me at once, and my breathing hitched. *No.*

'You sniffed around him like a dog in heat, even after I warned you not to hurt him—now look what you went and did. Exactly what I said not to. I don't know what happened between you two, but he didn't deserve that.'

'You're right.'

The blazing anger in her eyes softened just slightly.

'Go to the hospital. I'll stay here with Grace.'

She nodded, her anger replaced with concern over seeing Cohen. 'You'll be okay to get Grace off to school?'

'Just go.'

Her eyes searched mine for understanding. This was a woman who'd been through her fair share of heartbreak, and she seemed to understand that sometimes even the best of us fuck up. At least I hoped that was what she was thinking. Her words had been harsh, but worst of all, they were true.

Denise nodded again and grabbed her purse from the table before disappearing out the door.

I curled into a ball on their couch and cried myself to sleep.

Chapter 19

A few hours later I got Grace off to school, assuring her that everything was fine, even though I hadn't heard a peep from Denise. I swung by Cohen's to let Bob out and feed him, and then headed to my place to shower and change. I got back to the hospital around ten and was determined to see Cohen today, despite the hospital's strict family-only visiting policy. I cursed myself for not exchanging cell phone numbers with Denise. I called the only other person I could think of—my landlord, since he'd informed me of Cohen's accident in the first place, and thankfully he knew Cohen's hospital room number.

I found his room on the sixth floor, and lingered outside. I could see his mother through the small glass windowpane in the door and Cohen's sleeping form in the hospital bed, institutional-grade white sheet tucked in around him. He looked pale and had plastic IV tubes connected to the back of his hand, but otherwise okay. My knees knocked together, and I braced myself against the wall. He was okay. He was going to be all right.

The door opened a second later and Denise stood before me, frowning.

'How is he?'

She closed his door before addressing me so as not to disturb his sleep. 'He'll recover. He shattered his shoulder falling through

144

the floor and has a concussion and some bruised ribs, but otherwise, he'll be all right.'

'Can I see him?'

She released a long slow sigh. 'I don't think that's a good idea.'

I waited for her to continue, to tell me that I should come back when he was awake… something, anything, but she just stood there stoically.

'I know you two had sort of a falling out, and I'm not sure he'd want you to see him like this. Thank you for taking care of Grace. And Boo Boo. I've got it covered from here.' She disappeared back into his hospital room before I could formulate a response.

I bit down on my lip hard enough to draw blood to keep from myself from crying, but it did little good. Tears of frustration silently streamed down my cheeks.

I heard Cohen's muffled voice croak from inside the room. 'Who was that?'

'It was nobody, dear. Nobody at all,' Denise answered matter-of-factly.

And she was right. I had walked away from him because I was too afraid to admit what I was feeling. What was I feeling for him? Did I love him? If I couldn't even voice it in my own head, surely he didn't deserve to be strung along, and I escaped down the hall before I could mess anything up further.

Despite my lack of sleep and ragged condition after leaving the hospital, I drove straight through to my mother's house in Iowa. Though I hadn't been there more than twice in the past five years, I easily navigated I-90, avoiding the toll roads like I'd been doing it all the time.

During the first few hours of the drive, I argued with myself nonstop and nearly turned around half a dozen times, at one point even pulling into a rest stop to contemplate the decision. I refused to let Denise drive me away. More than anything, I wanted to be there for Cohen. But as the hours wore on, I came to believe that the right thing to do was to leave him be. He deserved more than what I had to offer. And once I explained it to myself that way—that I wasn't staying away because Denise had the power to push me around, but instead, because it was the best thing for Cohen—I instantly felt a little bit better and continued along to my Mom's house, knowing I would need to escape to the solace of home. Returning to my own home would bring too many reminders of Cohen.

I arrived at her home without even an overnight bag and was in her arms, crying like a baby, before I even stepped inside the house.

The visit with my mother was exactly what I needed. I'd never grieved Paul's death properly, and I spent the week in Iowa doing just that. I slept in each day like I'd been sleep deprived for years. I visited his grave for the first time and placed flowers on it. I overindulged on my mother's cooking and talked to her—actually opening up—about losing my fiancé, and my ability to have children. It was hard, but by the end of the week I felt stronger. And not just as the invented Liz I'd once used to cope, I was stronger as Eliza. Me. And it felt good.

I also realized that I missed Cohen. I missed eating our meals together, sleeping in his bed, even playing those damn video games I was so bad at. Cohen always saw through my act. He'd called me by my full name from the beginning, even when I kept insisting he call me Liz. It was like he'd somehow known the true me was inside the entire time.

When I rolled to a stop on the street in front of my townhouse, I thought I'd have more time to prepare before facing Cohen, to figure the right words to say, but there he stood with Bob on the sidewalk, his arm secured to his side in a sling, watching me get out of the car.

I gathered up the overnight bag of random stuff I'd accumulated when at my mom's. I'd left with nothing but the clothes on my back, and of course she'd taken me shopping, for some new clothes, shoes and makeup. Cohen watched my every move as I wrestled the large bag from the passenger seat.

Bob sat at Cohen's heels, but when I got near he charged forward, yanking the leash free from Cohen's grasp and charging straight for me.

I steered clear of Bob's path, grabbing his leash and returning it to Cohen's outstretched hand. 'How's your shoulder?' I nodded toward his arm, held immobile by the sling.

'Fine, as long as I don't move it. It should heal up nicely. But I can't respond to calls for the next eight weeks.'

I nodded. 'I'm glad to see you up and around.'

He squinted, looking unsure.

'It's just the last time I saw you, you were still unconscious after surgery,' I explained.

'You came to the hospital?' He eyed me warily.

'Of course. A couple of times. And I stayed with Grace so your mom could come that first night, and I took care of Bob too.'

The look on his face told me he was either mentally solving a long equation, or this information was entirely new to him.

Of course his mother didn't tell him. I took a step closer to him. 'I was there, Cohen. I wanted to see you, and your mom thought it was best... I mean, it probably was for the best that I just let you be.'

'Why would you say that? My mother doesn't know shit about what I want or need. I would have wanted to see you. That night with you was the best night of my life, and then after...when you took off...' He stopped abruptly, and looked down, his eyes burning with intensity.

'I'm sorry,' I managed in barely a whisper. I knew it wasn't the apology he deserved, but words seemed to be escaping me. I looked down at the sidewalk, all of my courage dissolving at the sight of him.

'You were scared,' he said.

I looked up and met his gaze. He was the same confident, beautiful man I'd fallen for, if not a bit more banged up and wary of me. It broke my heart to see him like this, knowing I was the cause of it.

He rubbed a hand across his stubble-roughened jaw then adjusted the strap on his sling. 'Come inside. We're not talking about this out on the street.'

I swallowed and nodded my consent.

We didn't even bother stopping at my place to drop off my bag, but instead I followed him and Bob up the stairs. I was sure my cats would be okay without me for a little while longer, Ashlyn always took good care of them when I was away. As we made our way up the stairs, I couldn't help but notice even Bob was acting different, like he could sense the tension between us, and his normally happy-go-lucky mood was replaced by one of calm.

When we reached his apartment Cohen freed Bob from the leash and then shrugged out of his sling, rolling his neck to shake off the aches and pains.

'Aren't you supposed to keep that on?' I looked at the discarded sling.

He nodded. 'Probably. It's uncomfortable though.'

Men could be such babies. I picked up the sling from the couch and folded it before setting it aside on the trunk in front of the sofa.

'Sit down. Do you want something? Water? Sorry, I don't have much else. Haven't been to the store in a while.'

The way he said it made me wonder if he'd been eating, and I imagined it'd be difficult to prepare meals one-handed.

'No, I'm fine.' I sat down on the opposite side of the sofa, keeping some distance between us.

Cohen tucked his arm against his side, so as not to jostle it, and sat down. 'So, I, um, talked to Ashlyn. I didn't know where you were staying, and she told me…some things about your past.'

A lump rose in my throat and I clenched my hands into fists. *Damn it, Ashlyn.*

'She didn't tell me much, said it was your story to tell, but just that I didn't know what you'd been though and not to judge you too harshly.'

I released the breath I'd been holding. 'Is that all she told you?'

He shook his head. 'She also said you're not as tough as you try to seem.'

I smiled wryly. Well, after the way I'd broken down this past week, I supposed that much was true.

He shifted closer to me on the sofa, closing some of the distance between us. 'So…' he prompted.

I chewed on my lip, deciding if I could tell him. This wasn't how I pictured it. I'd imagined I'd have time to prepare what I wanted to say, be dressed in something cute—hell, at least be showered—and maybe tell him over drinks to soften the blow. But I summoned my courage. It was either explain myself now, or lose Cohen forever. I cleared my throat and began. 'You deserve to know, I know that. And I want you to know that what you gave me, what we shared, it meant a lot to me too.'

He smiled and took my hand. 'Just say it. What could possibly be so bad, Easy E?'

I shifted away from him, uncomfortably. I couldn't allow myself to get my hopes up for him to just reject me in the end. It was the entire reason I'd tried to keep him at arm's length, and then pushed him away. I wrung my hands in my lap. 'I was engaged.' My eyes flicked to his, and they were concerned and curious, but not angry. Yet.

I took a fortifying breath, and told him the rest of the story, not once stopping or breezing by a single detail. Cohen stayed silent, holding my hand, waiting for me to get all the words out. He rubbed slow circles on the back of my hand with his thumb, not interrupting or asking any questions, just listening attentively. I was in tears by the time it was over.

I didn't realize quite when it happened, but Cohen had moved closer to comfort me and soothe away my tears, slowly stroking my back, quietly whispering that everything was going to be okay.

When I realized that Cohen hadn't pushed me away, repulsed or angry, or worst of all—emotionless over the fact I couldn't have children, indicating he couldn't see a future with me, all the tension of holding my secret in for so long finally melted away and I was left physically and emotionally drained. I curled against his warm body and snuggled into his neck, letting the tears come. Tears for Paul, for the baby we lost, for future little blonde-haired, blue-eyed babies with Cohen, for all of it. And when I was finally done, cried out and limp, Cohen picked me up from the sofa and carried me to bed, tucking me in and murmuring lovingly before turning off the lights and leaving me to rest.

Epilogue

One Year Later
Cohen

I stretched back in my beach chair, a bottle of beer dangling from one hand, watching Eliza splash in the frigid Lake Michigan waves with Bob. He was wagging his tail, biting at the water, but even his antics weren't enough to keep me from watching her every movement. Her soft curves filled out that little bikini in ways that should be illegal. The only reason I was okay with her wearing it in public was because technically we were on a private beach and Aiden and Ashlyn weren't bound to notice anything but each other at the moment anyways.

We'd all come up to the same lake house as last summer, only this year to mark my college graduation, and to celebrate with Ashlyn and Aiden who'd just returned from their two-week-long honeymoon in Fiji. Their wedding was simple, yet elegant and Eliza made a beautiful bridesmaid. I stood in as the best man, not because Aiden didn't have other friends—he did—it was just that his memories had never returned and he felt closer to those he'd met since developing amnesia.

I pulled back a swig of my beer as Bob shoved his snout in between her legs and she toppled over, falling with a splash onto her ass in the shallow water. I let out a chuckle and watched her

151

face go from surprise to irritation to a fit of laughter. She wiped her hair from her face and scolded Bob, though she was still smiling, so I knew she wasn't really mad. He'd really grown on her over the last year. Well, that and she'd really changed over the past year, becoming more loving, more spirited, and more at peace. It had been amazing to see.

Once she stood and brushed the sand from her bikini bottoms, she jogged toward me, her tits bouncing in the most hypnotic way. I knew I'd never get tired of her body, and something stirred inside of me once again at just the sight of her.

'Did you see what that oversized mutt did to me?' She settled onto my lap, dripping with freezing water.

The ice-cold water soaking my swim trunks took care of any desire I felt stirring. I lifted her off me and wrapped her in a towel before folding her onto my lap again. She smiled at the warmth of the sun-warmed towel and nuzzled into my chest. It was times like this I felt proud of her, of the way she battled and overcame her fear to allow herself to fall in love again.

'I'm going to shower,' she whispered in my ear. 'Want to join me?'

I pressed a kiss to her neck and nodded. 'Go start it, I'll be right up.'

She hopped onto her feet and dashed up the sandy beach toward the house.

I don't know why I was so damn nervous about this. I wiped my palms on my shorts, and paced in the loft. The shower had been running for ten minutes already, and though she liked long showers, I knew she was waiting for me to get in there.

Shower sex had become one of my favorite things. Then again, I had a lot of new favorite things where Eliza was concerned. We'd experimented with just about every position known to man and even a few I think we made up. Not to mention doing it in every room in both her place and mine. After waiting so long for the right girl, now that I had her, I couldn't get enough. And luckily, she felt the same way.

I took one last glance around the room, making sure everything was perfect, when I heard the water shut off. She was going to be ticked at me for not joining her, but hopefully she would understand why.

I could hear her slamming drawers and moving aggressively about the bathroom. Yep, she was pissed.

A few seconds later the door opened and Liz came out, hair brushed but wet, and wrapped up in a towel. I'd lit candles all around the room, so it was softly glowing in the fading afternoon light and I was sitting on the bottom bunk. These bunk beds were sort of nostalgic for us and I thought about how far we'd come together in a year.

My chest was bare, the way she liked me, and I was stripped down to just a pair of white boxer briefs that she bought for me, claiming they were sexy. I didn't know about that, all I knew was I felt like I was offering myself to her, and I guessed that was pretty much the truth.

The scowl on her face faded away and was replaced by confusion as she took in the room. 'Cohen?'

'Come here, baby.' I held out one hand and she walked toward me. I loved that despite everything in her past she trusted me completely with her whole heart.

A few months into us dating, she'd gotten too drunk out with Ashlyn one night and when she got home late, she'd come to my apartment and in her drunken state sort of admitted that she loved me. She kept patting the top of my head and calling me 'Coh Coh' and telling me I could never leave her. I knew what she was really saying—that she'd fallen in love with me, and couldn't go through losing another man she loved.

After that night, knowing she was mine, it took our relationship to a whole new level. We hadn't spent anymore nights apart, and though Eliza's cats weren't happy about the arrangement at first, the more she began bringing them upstairs with her, the more Bob grew on them. We'd worked through all her fears and insecurities, the biggest of which surprised me – her inability to carry a child. After that breakthrough, we'd spent hours together researching international adoption online and viewing pictures of the infants and children who desperately needed a loving home. Showing her I was very much open to the idea of adoption seemed to erase the last burden she'd been carrying around. We'd daydreamed about our future, traveling to Brazil, China, Russia, building a family our own way.

She reached the side of the bed and stood before me, wrapped in just a white towel. I tugged the tucked corner free and let the towel fall to the floor.

'What are you doing Coh...?'

I gripped the backs of her thighs, tugging her toward me. 'Shh. Come here. Make love to me.'

She crawled onto the bed, settling on my lap and kissed me.

The times when she turned herself over to me completely and became this softer version of herself leveled me. I could always tell that there was more to her—more to our relationship—from the very beginning, even when she didn't want there to be.

She wasted no time, tugging at my boxers, and blazing a trail of wet kisses down my stomach. I held myself still, rather than pushing my hips up to meet her waiting mouth—which was what I really wanted to do—and instead bit back a curse when her warm mouth closed around me.

God, I loved this girl.

I wrapped both my hands in her hair, lifting it away from her face, losing myself in the scent of her shampoo and the things she could do to me with that naughty mouth of hers.

Once she had me deliriously worked up, she pulled away and smiled up at me with swollen, damp lips. Her eyes held the hint of a challenge, and I slipped my hands under her arms, pulling her up toward me, and deposited her next to me. Then she opened her thighs and I was lost forever.

Later, when we were both thoroughly satisfied and exhausted, lying together in the rumpled sheets, I held her body against mine so we were face to face. She nestled even closer into my neck, curling herself against me, and I couldn't help but smile, noticing how perfectly she fit alongside me.

If I'd had any energy left in my body, I'd probably be nervous, but this just felt right. I reached one hand over the edge of the bed, to find the ring I'd tucked under the mattress. For a second I couldn't locate it, and I was sure she was about to notice what I was doing when my fingers grasped it. Once the ring was closed safely in my hand all of the puzzle pieces clicked together and I knew everything was right.

I laced my fingers with hers and brought her hand to my lips. 'Eliza Jane,' I pressed a kiss to her palm. 'I want you to be mine forever. Will you marry me?' I held the sparkling, one-carat ruby ring in the palm of my other hand. She looked at the ring, and then at me, and then at the ring again, and her eyes filled with tears. I chose a ruby rather than a diamond and I hoped she understood why. She was engaged once before, and of course Paul had given her the traditional diamond ring. I wanted something that was just ours, and red was her favorite color. But as I watched her eyes overflow with tears, I was worried I'd done the wrong thing.

A sob broke free from her chest and she threw her arms around my neck. 'Yes, yes,' she whispered, kissing my neck in between her murmurings. 'Yes, Cohen.'

I squeezed her back, just holding her while she cried. I knew I couldn't imagine all of the mixed emotions she was possibly feeling at that moment, but all I felt was happiness. 'I love you, Eliza,' I whispered.

'I love you, Cohen,' she whispered back.

I wiped the tears from her cheeks and slid the ring up over her knuckle. Seeing the happiness on her face at the sight of the ruby nestled on her finger pushed away all doubt that she liked the ring. She smiled as she looked down at it, turning her finger to refract the light against the deep-crimson gem and diamond-studded band. I loved seeing it on her, and even more than that, I loved seeing her this happy. My mom and Grace had approved of the ring and my plan, and it appeared they hadn't steered me wrong.

I brought her left hand to my mouth and pressed a kiss over her knuckles. 'Mine, forever.'

She cupped my cheek and nodded. 'Forever.'